THE TESLA PROJECT:
1975

The Tesla Project Series
Part I

Rod Galindo

v1.2

Wordwraith Books

ISBN-13: 978-0-9908743-4-8
ISBN-10: 0990874346

Wordwraith Books, LLC
705-B SE Melody Lane #147
Lee's Summit, MO 64063
www.wordwaiths.com
@Wordwraiths

Cover art by The Cover Collection
www.thecovercollection.com

Rod Galindo's website www.rodgalindo.com
Rod Galindo's Twitter @RodAGalindo

This story is dedicated to my fellow Wordwraiths. Were it not for this close-knit writing group, none of my wild ideas would ever have made it outside my small circle of friends.

Thank you for checking out my short story, I hope you enjoy it!

At the end of this novelette is the first three chapters of my upcoming novel "**Distress Call**", the first book in the "SENTCORPS" series. If you enjoy military science fiction, please take a look!

For more information on upcoming projects and books, please visit RodGalindo.com!

The Tesla Project: 1975

I

Sergeant First Class Mike Tyler touched his earpiece to activate the embedded microphone. "Raven Rock Command, this is Traveler Three, commo check, over."

"Roger, Traveler Three, read you Lima Charlie," came the tinny reply from a random technician, indicating the command center could hear him "loud and clear."

He adjusted the weight on his back, a modified U.S. Army-issue rucksack. It was half empty to allow room for to-be-acquired items but was still heavy, mainly thanks to the working guts of a mini rocketpack the U.S. Army of 2025 allowed him to bring back with him. Not to mention its fuel.

"All departments report GO," announced a civilian wearing a colorful shirt and even louder tie, sitting just over a hundred meters in front of Tyler in a theater-style room. The man and a dozen other military and civilian personnel sat or stood, viewing him through a narrow, rectangular window. "Traveler Three, Standby."

Director Johansen's voice boomed in his ear. "Traveler Three, you are authorized to load your weapons."

"Roger, RAVROCOM." He first loaded a thirty-round magazine into the standard Army-issue M-16 that his superiors all but forced him to take along, and "charged" the rifle to load a round into the chamber. He left the weapon on "Safe" because he didn't trust it; one violent bump and the damn thing had a habit of discharging on its own. He was about to take it through a rift in spacetime; he didn't want to imagine what throwing a piece of lead off into the quantum foam—he'd heard it called that once—might do to the universe. There were more trustworthy future upgrades of the rifle, such as the M-16A1, the M-16A2, and even the M-4 and its various incarnations; his fellow travelers had brought them back for study and he had seen American soldiers carrying them on his many trips to the future. But would General West allow him to use those? *Of course he won't.*

After much back and forth, he was finally allowed to keep his favorite pistol, a .50 caliber Desert Eagle he'd obtained from a trip to 2005. "Betty", as he called the satin-black Mark XIX, combined the power of a revolver with the characteristics of a rifle all soldiers were familiar with, the aforementioned standard Army-issue M-16. These attributes made it the most powerful semi-automatic pistol the world had seen, even up through 2025. He slapped a seven-round magazine into Betty and charged her to send a round into the chamber, but intentionally left the safety off; Tyler had no fear of Betty coughing up a round when he didn't want her to do so. He then re-holstered the ten-inch, polygonal-barreled hand cannon, built to bore through car engine blocks, and touched his earpiece again. "Ready."

"Roger, Traveler Three," replied the Director.

"Coordinates set," he heard someone announce. "Capacitors at ninety-nine percent. Supercoolers are GREEN. Initializing temporal core."

Tyler experienced a slight disorientation as the round platform he stood upon freed itself from the only physical object holding it in place—a long, thick chrome pillar, which was currently out of his sight. In his mind's eye he could see the pillar dropping into the lowest point of the sphere, one hundred meters beneath him. He steadied himself; now only powerful rare-Earth magnets in the platform kept it, and him, from plummeting over three hundred feet to the sea of lightning rods jutting up from below like stalagmites from a cavern floor. Hundreds of similar rods jutted from every direction he looked. A one-hundred-meter walkway to his right, leading to the platform upon which he stood, began its painfully slow retraction.

"Core at twenty percent," said the civilian in the technicolor shirt. "Thirty. Fifty. Supercoolers dipping slightly, still well within nominal levels."

The walkway clicked when it completed its journey into the wall just beneath the only door out of the huge spherical room.

"Initiating Relocation Gyros," said another tech.

Sergeant Tyler's heart pumped harder as three large, circular rings lifted from their resting place around the central platform, not unlike the rings around Saturn. They began to rotate around themselves, around *him*. The largest ring was so big, it spun only a few meters from the inner wall. The middle ring spun inside the large ring. The third and smallest ring was close, too close for Tyler's comfort. The result of this array was three rings spinning independently of each other, all on different vectors, in a dizzying dance. Tyler focused on the control room; he learned long ago not to look too long at those damned rings, they would just make him queasy.

A wind picked up, generated by the motion of the rings. Tyler's gaze rose to the lightning rods above him in anticipation. *There they are!* The blue-violet stars. He couldn't help but smile at the sight, as the tip of each rod all around the Temporal Sphere glowed with Saint Elmo's Fire in the dense magnetic field generated by the spinning blades. The "fire" created a buzzing that grew in intensity with the wind and made the breeze smell tinny from ionization.

"Translocation Gyros stable, speed at target parameters, Einstein-Rosen horizon rising," said the colorful civilian. "Transferring coordinates to TRM computer."

TRM. Time Relocation Mechanism. Mike Tyler often chuckled that something with such a name was actually a part of his duty description. Who would have ever guessed?

He had never been in a tornado, but he guessed this was what one felt like. A tiny one, at least. He pulled the bill of his helmet, or "Kevlar", down over his eyes and crouched to make himself a smaller target, less aerodynamic so as not to be swept off the platform.

A new voice filtered into his ear now. "Now's not the time to be sucking your thumb, Mike."

Tyler cocked his head slightly and eye-balled the far right end of the giant rectangular window before him. There stood his commander and friend, Major Matthew Wilson, observing the trip. "Asshole," he muttered without keying his mic.

He saw Wilson lean over and speak into one of the microphones. "Say again, Traveler Three, we didn't quite catch that." As usual Wilson wore his Army Class A dress uniform instead of the slightly dressed-down Class B which most other military personnel wore at the facility. His jacket and pants were impeccable, creased in all the right places. A stack of service and campaign ribbons, most of which he had been awarded for various tours to Vietnam, nearly reached his collarbone.

Tyler touched his earpiece this time to activate the microphone. "Just said I'm ready to go," he shouted, so as to be heard over the wind and the buzzing of the glowing rods.

Wilson laughed, silently from Tyler's perspective.

Director Johansen spoke into his ear now. "Sergeant Tyler, initiate hover mode. One-half thrust."

This marked a change in standard procedure. On every occasion before now, Tyler simply jumped through an open rift above the round platform like he was walking through a doorway. This time he was forced to do things a little differently. He opened a small green box on his heavy, olive-drab-green utility belt and removed what looked like the grip of a gun, minus the barrel. With his thumb he pressed the red glowing button on top of the hand grip and heard the click and whir of two gimbaling rocket nozzles extending from either side of his rucksack. He squeezed the trigger. The tiny rockets ignited, filling the sphere with light and exhaust. He mashed the trigger with more force, and his feet lifted from the ground. He listed sideways almost immediately. *Oh boy. Wilson was right, I should have practiced more.* He struggled to hover in one place over the windy platform.

"Steady, Mike!" he heard Wilson shout in his ear.

"I got it," he shouted back, fighting the handgrip, flying back and forth and forth and back, doing everything he could to keep himself mostly above the platform. At one point he turned his head just in the nick of time to prevent decapitation from one of the spinning rings and a very bad day for all involved.

"Open the rift now!" Wilson ordered.

"Not yet, sir," replied Johansen, "the core is only at..." he checked a readout. "Ninety-two percent. We need to be at least to ninety eight so the—"

"Open it before he's blown into those damned rings!"

Tyler heard nothing more, but could easily imagine the scowl on the Director's face. A second later, the inside edge of each spinning ring exploded with blinding white light. Before him grew the familiar swirl of a rip in spacetime. Blue smoky filaments extended from somewhere unseen around him and were then sucked into nowhere.

"Godspeed, my friend!" Wilson said in his ear. "If my older self greets you *this* time, tell that geezer it's time to retire, for Chrissakes!"

Tyler gave his commander a nod he wasn't sure was caught. He steered himself into the vortex before him. As usual, the world turned white, the most brilliant white he had ever experienced. It reminded Mike of the "Teller Light" that he read about, which occurred in the microseconds just after a nuclear explosion. A light brighter than the sun. He had once heard a rumor he couldn't quite believe, but which fascinated him nevertheless. It concerned what one of the scientists present at the Bikini Atoll detonation in 1954 said, the one without goggles who had his back to the mushroom cloud and was watching the other scientists. This man—Tyler couldn't remember his name—claimed that at the moment the "Castle Bravo" bomb went off, the flash of light was so bright that he could see the skull and jawbone of each man, as if seeing their heads in an x-ray image. The light was called the "Teller Light", after Edward Teller who had helped engineer the

U.S.A.'s first fifteen megaton "super" thermonuclear device.

But there was a much more groovy effect than ridiculously bright light during each 'jump'. Each time Tyler entered the cloud, the white world was there, but it always lingered much longer than it should. It was like watching a film in slow-motion, only he was in the film. He surmised that time itself slowed down as he traveled through the rift, but the scientists assigned to the Tesla Project didn't believe him. He had no proof; all the time-keeping instruments he took with him—including his watch—never strayed even a millisecond from those back in the project control room. For everyone else, his trip was instantaneous. For him, it lasted a good five seconds. He suspected this happened to the other travelers as well, but if so, they never admitted to it. In fact, they laughed at him when he brought it up. They called it "Tyler's Disney Land." Their teasing made Mike wonder if he was indeed crazy. Perhaps it didn't really happen, perhaps it *was* all just in his head.

Regardless if his Disney Land was real or not, he still wondered about the Teller Light. If someone were to ever go into the rift with him, would that person see Tyler's bones? And if so, would history call it the "Tyler Light", after the first guy to ever wonder about it?

A young enlisted man could dream.

Tyler was through. The crackling of the lightning remained, but the wind was gone. Before him was nothing but blackness. Tyler's head jerked from left to right, but nothing met his eyes save for tiny blue stars all around him, and occasionally a bolt of lightning danced from one point to another point behind him, presumably into the wormhole. Or was it the other way around?

The darkness was expected, but was still jarring and unusual, especially with his feet no longer planted on solid ground. He focused on the tiny blue stars, but had a hard way of telling if he was falling or zooming toward that inner wall ahead of him. He did his best to center the hand grip to ensure he had no trajectory of any kind, but it didn't help his nerves. He rotated the rocketpack's handgrip to the right, which rotated him 180 degrees. Now facing the opposite way, he found the red-tinted vortex exactly where it was supposed to be, which replaced the blue one from a moment ago. "There you are."

With it, he at least had solid bearings again, and a confirmation he was indeed motionless, hovering in mid-air. He tried to look past the dimly glowing red portal to 1975, which would remain open until closed by his friends back in that era. It swirled like cigarette smoke in a room with a draft. But other than it, he couldn't see much. The Temporal Sphere looked just like it had a few seconds ago, minus the spinning rings. The lightning rods here in this time all had the same blue-violet glow; the little stars that quieted his soul.

He caught something out of the corner of his eye. A patch of the sphere was illuminated below him.

He looked downward, but could see little past his body armor. He nudged the flight control stick forward, then made a slow bank to the left, flying around the vortex. This allowed him to turn his head to the left and look down. The rings were all there, stowed in place and motionless, as they should be, held in place by two giant mounts jutting from opposite walls. The inner ring was in his way, so he flew a little farther out, where he could see through the large gap between it and the middle ring. *There!* A single beam of light illuminated the lowest point of the sphere.

The camera.

The spotlight mounted to the large low-tech video camera the U.S. Army had sent into the Einstein-Rosen Bridge, or E-R Bridge, the day prior lay on the floor one hundred meters below him. Tyler reminded himself it had actually arrived here only seconds ago, relatively speaking, regardless of when it had been sent. The camera itself was in pieces, destroyed by the fall. No matter, it had done its job as pathfinder, saving *him* from being destroyed by the same fall. In the three seconds it had transmitted its video—yesterday by his frame of reference, only moments ago by its own—it had verified that any traveler would indeed need something to prevent a nasty fall if he or she were to survive more than three seconds on this trip. Hence the authorization to use the rocketpack this time.

Something crossed his mind. *The walkway.* He looked over his shoulder to find it retracted. *Odd.*

This was not standard operating procedure; when the blades had no reason to spin, as in the case of a receiving sphere, the walkway was always extended to the platform in the receiving time period. The platform was also always there to prevent a traveler from falling to his or her death. Looking more closely, he could make out the platform's outline on the floor; the camera had bounced off it when it made its crash landing.

Crash. This sparked alarm in Tyler's head. The Temporal Sphere was heavily insulated against sound, so the tearing noise generated by ripping the fabric of space and time, the crashing sound of the large camera, plus the roar of his rocketpack *could* have announced his arrival to anyone who might be in the immediate area outside the sphere, but not elsewhere in the facility. But thanks to the large rectangular window—which was actually six inches of clear metal rather than actual glass—the sphere did *not* insulate against visible light. And his rocketpack was generating a lot of light right now. His head snapped toward the control room. Enough light shone in there that he could easily make out familiar chairs and consoles. So could anyone else either in there or in the hallway off the control room, especially if the door to the hall was open and they happened to be anywhere near the sphere. It was time to head for the exit and minimize his "noise and light pollution."

Using slight movements of the grip, he steered himself toward the door. A wire-mesh catwalk ran around the equator of the room, just as it had in

1975, and was wide enough for two people to stand next to each other comfortably. Releasing the trigger, his right foot touched down on the catwalk, then his left. He pressed the red button on the handgrip again, and the small rockets cut off and snapped back into his ruck. Tyler assumed a crouched fighting stance and raised his rifle. He ceased all movements and listened. Nothing stirred except the gentle "breathing" of the still-open E-R Bridge, and the occasional crackle of electricity. Now only blackness filled the glass of the control room. A clap of thunder created by a rather nasty static discharge snapped him from his trance.

Tyler keyed his mic. "Raven Rock Command, this is Traveler Three, over."

"The...he is!" he heard someone say. It sounded like Director Johansen.

Major Wilson broke in. "Tra...ler Three, this is RAVR...OM, we read y..." The transmission was broken, but readable. "Gla... you made......ere safe. SITREP."

Tyler understood Wilson wanted a report on his situation. "Roger, RAVROCOM. I made it here in better shape than the camera did, that's for sure," Tyler said. "SITREP follows: Currently in the Temporal Sphere. Both the sphere and Control Room are dark and dusty, no power. The air is stale but breathable. No sign of hostiles. Or friendlies for that matter. Preparing to cut through the door to the sphere and explore the facility and surrounding area. How copy?"

"Rog........Traveler Three. Copy: sphere is...thout power, environme...al condition GREEN, prepp...ing to explore facil... Be advised, portal...re-open...cisely at 1500."

Tyler checked his digital watch. It read "11:03 18 MAY 75." He had just under four hours to find out what he could about this era and get back to the sphere to return home. Lieutenant Stark gave him very detailed instructions in the mission brief yesterday. *More like pounded them into my head.* His thumb engaged the mic. "Roger."

"No sign of......older self anywhe...?" asked Wilson, breaking standard radio protocol.

"Negative," Tyler replied.

"I'll take that as...ood sign; mayb......old bugger...inally retired!"

"Or he's kicked it."

Wilson ignored that. "Goo...luck, Mike, see you in four ho......AVROCOM out."

A second later, Tyler heard a deep *puff*. He glanced over his shoulder to see the glowing red smoke dissipate into the darkness at the center of the sphere and one by one, the tiny bluish flames on each lightning rod winked out. He was now immersed in total darkness, and was very much on his own.

Tyler pulled a MagLite from his belt and switched it on. Eight LEDs manufactured in 2025 projected their hyper-bright particles and waves around the room before he could cup the business end. "Dammit," he said under his breath. He shone his light on the sealed, metal door. Leaning the M-16 in the dark corner that the doorjamb and the thick wall of the sphere created, he dropped his rucksack and wedged the rifle between it and the wall. He removed a small cutting torch from a small side pocket of the ruck. At the touch of a switch, the torch ignited with a loud *powww*, and he got to work.

It took him just under four minutes to cut a semi-circular "mouse" hole, starting at the floor and working its way up on either side to about his waist. Using his revered "Thinsulate" gloves he'd picked up in some time period he couldn't remember now, he tried to grab the hot edges before the cut section fell.

He failed. The *thud* the piece made when it landed in the hallway beyond surely woke the dead. Tyler cursed himself. He immediately pulled Betty and crept forward into the dark, sweeping his powerful flashlight quickly to his left and right. He crouched again and waited, listening.

The wide hallway looked much like he remembered from his own time—a linoleum floor, tile walls and a rock ceiling—but it was unlit. He had never seen it dark before. He looked up to find overhead lights mounted every ten feet or so, but they were different than he remembered. Fancier, updated. The hall extended hundreds of meters in either direction, far past the reach of his beam. He peered into the blackness to his right, which was roughly Southwest, and held his breath. No sound. He spun his light to the left, Northeast, and repeated the process. A single drip of water reached his ears. Likely the nearby Industrial Water Reservoir to the Northeast, he reasoned. Satisfied he was alone, he started in that direction. He soon reached the control room, which was just up ahead on his left.

Tyler opened the door to the large, movie theater-stepped control room and shone his light inside. It looked no different than he remembered, with the exception that all the computers were shut down and the room was an overall dingy gray, what with all the terminals and furniture covered with the dust of years. He was about to step inside when he heard a click from somewhere to his right, further down the cavernous hall. Another drip of water? Two more clicks came. *Not water.* He jerked his flashlight and pistol in that direction. Nothing appeared out of the ordinary, and now the silence had returned. *Rats?* he mused. He hoped they weren't oversized versions like in the old science fiction films, turned into man-eating monsters thanks to radiation exposure after a nuclear war, or something equally as silly. Ignoring the noise, he shone his light back into the control room. From the entryway, it did not appear anyone had set foot in the room in at least—

More clicks, louder now. His head snapped back to the right, Betty and the beam aimed far down the hallway. He saw nothing. He took a step forward, and a distant, soft low growl reached his ears.

He froze. *Is that a dog?* More clicking noises. Possibly the tapping of claws on the linoleum? *Is it coming my way?*

Click, click, click. Silence. *Click, click.* Silence again.

"Hey pooch," he called. His voice echoed in the cave. "Listen, I don't have any food! Not for you, anyway. Go on, get outta here! I've got a job to do and not a lot of time to do it. So, go on! Scat!" he shouted.

The growl transformed into a snarl, and Tyler strove to find its source. He squinted and shone his light on every object and door he walked by. Some doors were closed. Those he ignored. The dark, dimensionless, open rooms were another story, and filled his gut with a foreboding of dark things waiting inside. They could harbor furniture, computers, or any manner of equipment. Or his worst nightmare. Or nothing.

The clicking resumed, and Tyler now located a direction of origin. Straight ahead. He discerned a repetitive pattern now, which echoed off the walls. He focused on the farthest point in the long, straight tunnel. His beam glinted off something shiny. An urge to shoot rose within him, but he pushed it down. What if it was a person? Or a robot that might be useful?

"Hello?" he called.

The growling intensified, and so did the clicking— or rather, the *galloping*. The foreboding rose from his gut to his throat. He swallowed, aimed, and squeezed the trigger at the approaching danger. A spark flew off into the darkness. The galloping and growling continued. He fired again. *Another spark?*

He could see the shiny object's shape now. It was a dog. But not a normal dog. Something inside screamed at him: *run.*

He ran.

In seconds, the hole he had cut only minutes ago was on his right, and he dove through it. He rolled to his left and ended up on his back, his head dangling off the wire-mesh catwalk as the dog burst through behind him. Its claws tore at the metal beneath it, the screeching sending shivers down Tyler's spine, but the creature's momentum was too great. It sailed off the catwalk, snarling all the way to the bottom. Tyler only had to wait a couple of seconds for the impact, and the sound was like nothing he was expecting. Instead of a thump and a final yelp before death, he heard the sound of a small locomotive ripping through a building. His brows came together. "What the hell?" He rolled over onto his stomach and directed his beam of light into the dark depths of the sphere.

He saw a long gouge cut in the pattern of lightning rods, starting from a point directly beneath him to nearly the lowest point of the sphere where the round platform sat. A shiny, metal shape reflected the light at the end of the swath. It looked like a dog, but it was not like any he had ever seen. Overall it had a dark charcoal coat, but there was no fur, just smooth, shiny skin, scratched and dented. Metal legs. Eyes with no pupils. His breath caught in his throat when he realized the thing was peering up at him. Noises reached his ears. Scrapes. Clicks. And then it lifted itself up.

Tyler stared, his brain not quite registering what his eyes reported.

It was still alive, despite a one-hundred-meter fall. Its left rear leg jutted off at an odd angle and appeared broken. The thing let loose a long howl that echoed across the large chamber. It sounded exactly like a living animal; there were no mechanical characteristics in its voice at all. A second later, it leaped into the sea of still-intact rods to its left, and began negotiating a path through them. Using them to climb the wall of the sphere.

"Oh, shit."

Sergeant Tyler wasted no time. He unholstered Betty, maneuvered his body farther over the edge of the catwalk to free his firing arm, and unleashed a rain of .50 caliber bullets directly into the robot. Traveling at speeds over 1,600 feet per second with nearly 2,000 foot-pounds of muzzle energy, he expected each hollow-tipped, 350-grain round to open a hole the size of a quarter on this side of the animal's head, and a small canyon on the other. Instead the rounds only bounced off the dog like Tyler had been tossing his failed, crumpled-up Economics tests in its direction. Nevertheless, he kept firing until Betty clicked, her magazine empty. The dog was still climbing.

And gaining speed.

Tyler looked over his shoulder and located his rucksack leaning against the wall on the far side of the large doorway. He dove for it, dropped Betty, shoved the end of the flashlight in his mouth, and dug two metal balls from an outer pocket. Holding one five-second grenade in each hand, he returned to the edge of the catwalk and lay again on his stomach, using his lips to aim the L.E.D. beam. The beast was now about fifty meters below, but not directly beneath him due to the curve of the sphere. It would make aiming more difficult, but not much. He pulled the pin on the first grenade, gripped the MagLite between his teeth and shouted, "Hey!" The dog's head raised a bit, and Tyler released the grenade's spoon. *One thousand one....* He tossed the little round explosive outward.

His aim was as perfect as he could have hoped for. With a roar, the dog caught the small ball in its mouth and bit down. Tyler spun and dove for the small opening in the door, still clutching the second grenade. He had just passed the threshold when the boom and shock wave thundered through his body. Debris clinked and tinked behind him. He crawled back to the catwalk and projected his beam through the wire mesh to verify the beast below was no longer a threat. The side of the dog's head was flowered open, half of it missing. Sparks shot from the gaping wound.

"Well, look who's not so tough now! That'll teach you to play fetch with a grenade! Dumb dog."

As if in answer, the thing turned to look at him with its one good eye. It let loose a low growl, then another howl, and the metal monstrosity began climbing again.

Tyler's mouth fell open. "You gotta be kiddin' me, man!" He scooted to the edge of the see-through catwalk, pulled the pin on the other grenade and reached far out over the edge. He let the spoon pop off and fall downward. Tyler reached "one thousand two" this time before he let the ball fall straight down, then dove for the hallway. He heard the grenade bounce twice before detonating.

This explosion was just as powerful as the one before it. He waited for all the debris to stop falling before crawling back through the door and perching again on the catwalk. He peered downward. The dog was in another location now, further to his right, amongst more broken lightning rods. One front leg was separated from the rest of the body, and other parts of the ersatz animal seemed in need of some untwisting and a good spit shine. But the thing was *still* moving, squirming in place.

"Christ, what are you made of?" he shouted at the thing. *At least it wasn't climbing anymore.* Tyler pushed himself up and sat back on his haunches, staring downward. He would need to return to this room in less than four hours. *If this dog stays where it is, and it doesn't have any missiles or guns built into it, it shouldn't matter,* he reasoned. *I can use my rocketpack to fly from here into the vortex in the center of the sphere, and just let sleeping dogs lie.* He chuckled to himself at the pun.

"You seem familiar to me, you know that, pooch? Something from a book or something. Can't quite place it..." His mind wandered as he retrieved Betty, dropped the empty magazine and fished a fresh one from his belt. He rammed it into the handle and let the slide slam forward. He then positioned his Kevlar atop his bulky rucksack in a way he was certain the helmet wouldn't slide off. Lastly, he ran four fingers through his tuft of brown hair to undo the matting job it had done. "Okay. Let's try this again," he muttered to himself. As he re-entered the dark tunnel, he could hear the mechanical monster's gears softly whirring, making every effort to finish its job.

To finish *him.*

Tyler made his way through the dark tunnels with his small but powerful MagLite and his memory as his guide. After working in the facility the last four years, he could see a map of the sprawling mountain complex in his head. The TRM sphere, the control room, and related offices were located in a recently-dug section near the West Power Plant. It wasn't far from the Industrial Water Reservoir, but it was a good five minute walk to the three-story, underground Building B where his barracks room was located. He didn't often sleep there, but after long missions, it was a nice place to shower and lay his throbbing head a while. He wondered who it was assigned to now, or if his key would still work in the door, or if Building B even housed barracks a century after he last saw his room.

It was quite a hike to any of the four "portals" leading out of the complex—the main entrances and exits to the outside world. But after his encounter with the nearly unstoppable robot dog, Tyler dared not try his luck with any of those. Fortunately, he didn't have to; an alternate exit was decided upon by his superiors only yesterday, when the camera's demise told them something was amiss in 2075. He and Betty "cleared" the tunnels, halls and nearby offices with speed and agility on his way to his destination: one of three little-used vertical maintenance corridors that doubled as emergency exits and led all the way to the surface, several hundred meters straight up. If it was a long walk to the portals, it was going to be an even longer climb. Not because of the distance, but simply due to the hundreds of stairs he would have to negotiate. It was Lieutenant Stark who assured him there were "landings" along the way for a person to catch his breath. Mike hadn't mentioned it to anyone, but he hoped there were several of them.

Back in 1975, the hatch would have opened into somewhat dense, deciduous woods on top of the Pennsylvania mountain. It was assumed it still did in 2075. The woods wouldn't offer much cover from possible incoming fire, but they should provide at least partial concealment from airborne or space-borne eyes. He hoped so anyway, and long enough for him to figure out a way to get from the mountain to Washington, D.C., about seventy miles to the South as the crow flies. Or at least to a nearby town. Perhaps Blue Ridge Summit, a relatively quick five-mile hike away? Maybe he could find a newspaper or a friendly local who could shed some light on things?

He reached the vertical corridor without incident. Nothing greeted him but a lot of musty air and dust, which made him cough. Tyler found the non-descript door to the corridor in a small alcove off one of the caverns. It was unlocked, much to his relief. He didn't fancy having to shoot a lock off and risk alerting any more hostile machines of his presence. It opened into darkness, but his MagLite found the steel staircase he was expecting. Holstering Betty, he started his long climb. He counted nine landings. At number four, he paused a few minutes to rest his legs and check his watch. "11:54." *Three hours.* At number seven, he paused again and ate two granola bars one newly-promoted Lieutenant Colonel Wilson had given him in 2015 for a "rainy day". They were small but satisfying.

The hatch at the top of the tall staircase was a welcome sight. He turned the mechanism that unlatched it, and the small rectangular door squeaked open on a spring-fed hinge. It was heavy. He lifted it with his back, and dirt fell into his face. He sputtered and shook dry leaves and caked dirt off him, then used all that was left of his energy to lift open the heavy door. He pushed until it locked into place with a loud *thunk*. His eyes had already adjusted to the darkness, and he had to squint in the noontime sun.

Unholstering his trusty sidearm, he climbed up and out of the abandoned Raven Rock Mountain Complex, or "Site R" as some called it. Betty had failed him thus far, but it was his only protection besides his M-16, which he had left back in the sphere. If Betty's .50 caliber hollow-tipped rounds couldn't handle things, the rifle's 5.56mm—or .223 caliber standard rounds—would not make a bit of difference. He remained low, scanning the trees around him. Everything *seemed* quiet, but something told him that someone—or something—was nearby. He couldn't hear or see it, but his senses told him the—

Motion to his left made his head and Betty both jerk in that direction. Not even a second later, his throat seized without warning and every muscle in his body contracted as a severe electric shock froze him from head to toe. Betty fired her chambered bullet without his consent. His teeth clenched like they were trying to mash themselves into a single piece of enamel. His eyes fought their sockets, trying to burst from his head. He couldn't think, couldn't breathe, he felt frozen in time. Then the buzzing assaulting his nervous system was gone, and he collapsed, but a tingling sensation still zipped through every fiber of his being.

Tyler sucked air, trying to catch his breath. With every bit of his might, he pointed a shaking Betty toward whatever had done this to him. A slight patch of forest, man-shaped, moved about ten meters away. Tyler put every ounce of his might into squeezing Betty's trigger, but nothing happened. He tried again.

Lightning flew out of the strange patch of forest and enveloped his body, but only for half a second this time, not the eternity it seemingly had a moment ago. Betty thumped into the dirt near Tyler's head. He managed a single, offensive word.

In the blink of an eye, the moving piece of forest resolved into a person—a girl with a brown pony tail. She had a small device in one hand—a gun of some kind—and a large, nasty-looking rifle on her back. "You should watch your language," she said.

Then everything went black.

II

Sounds. Voices. Warmth. Pain. Tyler pried his eyelids open, enough to allow searing light to burn his retinas. He slammed them shut again.

"Don't worry," said a gravelly voice. "The effects will wear off shortly." Then, "What setting did you say you used again, Hannah?"

"I already told you, Pawpaw. Five," said another voice, this one much more soft and feminine than the first. Full of youth.

Tyler choked out, "Who..? What..?"

"Relax, Mike," said the man. "You're among friends."

At the sound of his name, Tyler's eyes shot open. The light hurt and made him blink and squint, but he was determined to find out who was holding him prisoner. He caught a glimpse of two shadows—no, three—all hovering above him. He focused on the larger one, which seemed closest. "How do you know my name?" he spat.

"Mike. It's me."

Tyler squinted through fluttering eyelids. The eyes of an ancient man with a white beard stared back at him. He didn't recognize the face, but he knew those eyes. "Major Wilson?"

"*Colonel* Wilson, thank you very much!" said the old man. "But you can call me Matt now. I haven't been called 'Colonel' in nearly seventy-five years. Well, not since recent days, anyway."

"Dad?" said a third voice. "Here."

Wilson turned. "Ah, thank you, Amber." A cup was put to Tyler's lips. "Here. Drink."

He did. The liquid was cool and tasted like bitter water. It had an odd smell as well. He didn't care; he swallowed and took another sip, then grabbed the cup and drank the rest. He cleared his throat and lay his head back down. After a moment, he decided he could finally speak normally. "What did you do to me?"

"My great granddaughter here used a stun gun on you."

"A what?"

"It's like an electronic tranquilizer. We didn't mean—"

"Why?"

"You were about to shoot me!" barked Hannah.

Tyler lifted his head and forced his eyes to work. The old man's features then came into focus and he jerked back.

"My apologies, Mike, if my appearance startles you. These last hundred years have been hard on me. Hard on all of us."

"A hundred years! Well that means you must be..." He tried to do math in his head, but couldn't make the numbers make sense.

"Medical science has grown by leaps and bounds since 1975, Mike! At least it did before the war."

Tyler jabbed his fingers into his left temple and clenched his eyes and jaw shut.

"You'll feel like your old self soon, Mike," assured Wilson.

Tyler opened his eyes and saw two women standing behind the old man. One was tall with long, salt and pepper hair. *Amber,* Tyler thought he remembered Wilson calling her. The other was a pony-tailed teenager who stood with crossed arms and a cold stare. She had a familiarity about her, but then both women did. Something in the eyes... Then it hit him. The genes on the Wilson side of the family were strong. "Let me guess," he said. "Fruit of your loins?"

"What did he just say?"

"Give him a break, girls," Tyler heard Wilson say. "He's from another time. We were more... crude back then."

Crude? Tyler thought, but decided to ignore it. "A full Colonel, huh? Last I saw you, in 2025, you were still an L-T-C." Meaning a Lieutenant Colonel.

"Eh, they'll promote anyone who keeps his nose clean and his jimmy in his pants. Sorry, girls," he added.

Amber turned away.

"Who'd you marry, anyway?" asked Tyler. "Anyone I know?"

"Well, actually," replied Wilson, "it's kind of an amusing story. You see—"

"*You.*" Tyler aimed his own cold stare at Hannah, who had barely moved a muscle since he first saw her. "You're the one who shot me, aren't you?"

The younger girl said nothing.

"Why didn't you just say, 'Hi, how are ya? I'm Colonel Wilson's granddaughter, you must be Sergeant Tyler, it's nice to meet you.'?"

"*Great* granddaughter," Hannah corrected. "And you had a giant gun with actual bullets pointed at my head, *Sergeant*." She emphasized his title, as if berating him.

"I had no idea you were just some little girl!"

"Just some little girl!?" she shouted, and advanced on him.

Wilson held up a hand and Hannah came to a halt.

"Hell I didn't know what you were!" Mike said, spewing the words as best he could. "You looked like a moving *tree* to me. I was afraid you were a camouflaged dog or something!"

Silence fell upon the group.

"A dog?" asked Wilson.

"Those mechanical jobs you've got creeping around this place."

"A Hellhound?" asked Amber. "But how could you possibly know about—"

"Yes!" exclaimed Tyler. "Hellhound! That's what's they're called! From—"

"*Fahrenheit 451*," Wilson said with him in unison.

Tyler smiled and nodded. "Couldn't remember that for the life of me."

"Yeah, yeah, we all read the book," Hannah interrupted. "Answer my grandma."

"What's the question again?"

The girl let out a deep breath. "How do you know about the Hellhounds? Pawpaw said you were from 1975. They weren't invented until, what, fifteen, twenty years ago?"

Wilson nodded. "Right around the year you were born, Hannah."

"I met one," said Tyler. "It wasn't a good first date."

"You met one?" exclaimed Amber. "How'd you kill it?"

"I didn't kill it, it's still alive. Or whatever you call a robot that's not dead. I fired a whole mag of fifty cal rounds right into that damned thing, and they bounced off it like BBs. Had to use grenades."

"But if it's still alive..." Amber began.

Wilson spoke up. "Mike, where is it?"

"It's trapped at the bottom of the Temporal Sphere."

"It's okay," said Wilson, "it can't broadcast from inside the sphere."

Hannah's eyes were wide. "How'd you get it down there?"

"Well, I kinda tricked it. I went this way, it went that way and..." He made a whistling sound that started high and ended low, to portray something falling off a cliff. "...Boom! And man, it was a *big* boom. Sounded like a freight train hit the bottom. That's when I first realized it wasn't just a mean old junkyard dog. It's probably still there," he continued. "I tore it up pretty good. Tore off one leg, broke another, ended up with only half a head. But the beast was still tryin' to crawl out! I was out of grenades, so I high-tailed it outta there." He looked at Wilson. "I told you—the younger you, I mean—I should always carry at least six!"

Hannah stared at Tyler with doe eyes. "Wow," she whispered.

"Amazing," said Wilson. "You were incredibly lucky. So, it was waiting for you when you came through the wormhole?"

"No, I met it in the tunnel outside the sphere. It chased me back in there."

Amber and Wilson looked at each other, their eyes betraying an emotion Tyler couldn't quite nail down.

"If it was outside the sphere, then it was surely in contact with its base!" Amber pointed out. A second later, she was scurrying about, collecting equipment.

"I don't understand," said Tyler.

Wilson stood and took a few steps toward a small crate. "Mike, these dogs and drones are in constant communication with one another and their headquarters. The sphere would block the signal, but if it was in the tunnel when it saw you… Well, within the hour we're going to have that puppy's friends beating down our door."

"But that tunnel's still what, three, four hundred meters under the mountain?"

"Doesn't matter. They can use a trail of radio relays to reach the surface."

Tyler's head pounded again. "Uh oh."

"Lieutenant Torres, Lieutenant Washburne," Wilson announced loudly, to seemingly no one. "Ready your men, we may have been reported by a lone hound Sergeant Tyler encountered in the complex." He spoke softly once more. "This could be more of an ordeal than I had hoped." He retrieved something from the crate and walked back over to Tyler. "Here's your girlfriend back." He held Betty out at arm's length.

Tyler smiled and took the gun. Wilson must have cleaned her up for him, because last time he saw her she was lying next to his head, blasphemously on the dusty ground. He checked the magazine. Six rounds left of seven; he remembered firing one in the forest when Hannah shot him. Can I have my ammo back?"

"Can you walk?" Wilson asked.

"I probably don't have much of a choice, do I?"

"Not anymore." The old man held up Tyler's lightweight armor, which held several magazines of .50 caliber ammunition in its front pouches, along with four 7.62 magazines he didn't need. "Had you not encountered that Hellhound, this could have been a leisurely stroll. I was planning on spending these four short hours I have with you catching you up on all that's happened since I last saw you. Now I'll have to squeeze in what I can while dealing with what Rommel might throw at us."

Rommel? Mike's mind heaved. *Surely not Hitler's Field Marshal of the early 1940s.* The mysterious quantum rules of the cosmos prevented some impossible possibilities. Like the steadfast one barring travel to and from a time before the machine was built. And it was built in 1965, long after World War II. *Or so I was told.* "Colonel, please tell me it's not actually—"

"Later," Wilson assured him, helping Tyler don his armored vest. "Right now we need to move. And as silently and as quickly as we possibly can."

III

Tyler was told the hatch leading back into the Raven Rock facility was about four hundred meters up the side of the mountain from where the group was currently located; the camp where he had awoken after being stunned by Hannah. Two infantry platoons consisting of about thirty men and women each had since materialized around the immediate area. He suspected the troops had been using some kind of camouflage that employed light-bending technology. When activated, only the soldiers' outlines could be seen, and only if they moved. *We could sure use that kind of tech in Vietnam.*

The Lieutenant of First Platoon called "SP"—the Army's code for crossing the "Starting Point"—and the formation moved out at a "route-step" toward the access hatch under a canopy of majestic trees above. This was faster than a normal marching pace, and Tyler struggled to keep up in his condition. Sunlight lit up small patches of dead leaves and dry, bare ground every few meters. Every now and again, through the branches, he caught a glimpse of the red and white radio tower perched on top of Raven Rock mountain, known only as "Site R-T." As Tyler huffed and puffed and did his best not to ruffle the dry carpet of leaves, he wondered what the "R-T" stood for, and chuckled to himself. He didn't even know what the "R" in "Site R" stood for, and he worked there on a daily basis! Surely there was some rhyme or reason to the Army's naming convention, he simply had no idea what it was.

Mike caught Hannah looking in his direction. "Can I help you, miss?" he asked with a tone. He may have been more polite, but the sting of her "stun gun" still resonated in every last one of his nerve endings. It was because of her he was having difficulty keeping up with the soldiers around him.

"I still can't believe you single-handedly beat a Hellhound."

"Yeah? Well I may not have. Like I said it was still squirming around when I left."

"Still," the girl said, "it's pretty impressive. Especially for someone who comes from a world a hundred years removed from ours."

Wilson interjected. "Sergeant Tyler here is Army Special Forces. We even had a Navy SEAL on our original team. We were the U.S.A.'s 'cream of the crop' once upon a time."

"I know," said Hannah, rolling her eyes. "You won't let me forget it."

"Once upon a time?" Tyler smirked. "Speak for yourself."

Wilson laughed. "That's right; to you Mike, we're still that all-powerful, unbeatable force! To me, that was a lifetime ago. Several lifetimes ago. I had a family, watched my kids grow up and have kids of their own, and watched those children have children. Speaking of which, believe it or not,

Hannah here has gone up against several of those metal beasties herself!" He beamed with pride.

"Yeah, well, never *all by* myself." she corrected.

Wilson shook his head. "Don't let her fool ya, Mike, she's one helluva fighter."

"Colonel!" called a soldier, jogging up to Wilson.

"Yes, Lieutenant?"

The officer waited to speak again until he had arrived in front of his commanding officer and could speak more softly. "One of my men just reported another drone fly-by about three clicks to the Northwest."

"Are the jammers still functioning?"

"Yes, sir, but we don't want to be out in the open too much longer."

"Roger," said the old man. "Can we move faster, Mike?"

Tyler nodded. "Sure." He didn't mention the tingling zips that were shooting from toe to hip every step of the way.

"Let's get up this mountain, L-T."

"Roger, Colonel," acknowledged the Lieutenant, and made a hand-and-arm motion that told everyone to double-time to their objective: the access hatch.

Tyler's body screamed. But he'd be damned if he'd show weakness in front of these troops. He had stayed on-mission in Vietnam after a stray bullet found his arm, and he would stay the course now. Thankfully, the group reached the hatch in short order. First platoon poured down the staircase with a speed that amazed even Tyler. The

Wilson women climbed down next, followed by Mike and the Colonel.

A few steps down, Wilson spoke into the air. "Lieutenant Torres, once your platoon is inside, close and lock the hatch behind you." Before they had made their way to the second landing, he spoke again. "Roger, Torres! Lieutenant Washburne, we're all inside the facility. We'll rendezvous just outside the door to the vertical corridor."

The trip down was much faster. Tyler's legs burned, however, from the long trek up these very stairs not an hour before. Added to that the lingering pain of the stun gun, and it didn't make for a pleasant trip, even with gravity on his side this time.

At the bottom, the two platoons filed into the alcove and spread into a nearby tunnel. The soldiers silently took up defensive positions.

"Begin movement to the sphere, Lieutenant Washburne." Then to Tyler, "Mike, after you."

The group maneuvered tactically through the complex, rounding corners at Wilson's direction. The tingling in Tyler's body was starting to subside. "How long has this place been locked up?" he asked.

"Just shy of a hundred years," said the Colonel.

"*What?*"

"It was closed up in May, about a month or so after you left." Wilson sighed. "The Powers-That-Be just couldn't justify leaving the program running. After the business with losing you, and then in April, when Saigon fell to the—" He abruptly stopped talking and lowered his gaze.

"Losing me?" asked Tyler. "What do you mean, losing me? And Colonel, hold on, you're not telling me we lost Vietnam are you?"

Wilson inhaled deeply, then smiled at Tyler. "I told you it's Matt. And I'll tell you everything when we get to the sphere."

"There's no way I can call you 'Matt'. But wait, if this place has been closed up for that long, none of these people have ever been in here, have they?"

Wilson shook his head. "I drew a rudimentary map which I put a close-hold on. I had the Platoon Leaders memorize it, then I destroyed it, just like I destroyed all the paper and digital blueprints I could find concerning this place."

"I see."

"Mike, I meant to be waiting for you on the walkway, as usual, when you arrived through the wormhole. But unfortunately, that hatch was locked up tight, and there was no way to get to any of the entrance portals without being seen. Portals C and D were obliterated in the war. A and B were under surveillance by—"

"L-T, we have incoming!" This from one of the two communications men.

"Distance, direction, speed, number?" the Second Platoon Leader boomed.

The soldier spoke softly into his headset. It seemed to take forever, but he finally spoke. "Charlie Company reports a large force about ten clicks South, heading for Site R," he reported.

"Moving at approximately sixty kilometers per hour!"

"Men from Rommel's Army?" asked Tyler.

"Men can't move that fast, not even in 2075," replied Wilson. "No, it's likely hounds. Possibly drones as well. But yes, sent from D.C."

"Hey man, what the hell *is* a drone, anyway?"

"Another *DARPA* project that was going on at the same time we were playing Time Lord with the sphere."

Tyler was aware the **Defense Advanced Research Projects Agency, or D.A.R.P.A.**, had their fingers in a slew of secretive projects. He knew of three. Two due to his clearance and "need-to-know." Another he had heard about of through the grape vine but wasn't sure he believed. But then, once again, he had to remind himself that a "temporal sphere" was a commonplace item in his professional career.

"How far to the sphere?" asked Amber.

"Not far," said Wilson. "We need to move!"

As old as he was, even the Colonel ran. In another few minutes, the group arrived in the linoleum hallway near the sphere, and slowed to a march. As each troop, man and woman caught their breath, Tyler had a few moments to study the soldiers' weapons. He saddled up close to one of them. "What kind of ammo does that fire, Private?"

"Phased plasma pulse, Sergeant," the young man replied. "One-hundred-fifty watts."

The boy might as well have been speaking Klingon. Tyler stepped over to Wilson. "What did he just say?"

"It's a laser gun."

"Oh. So when am I going to get a laser gun?"

"You're not getting any more future tech to take home with you. That could be what accelerated this entire political mess we're in now."

"Mess? What mess?"

Wilson turned to Amber. "How much time before the rift?"

She checked her watch. "Just under two hours."

The old man sighed. "I honestly don't know if we'll make it that long."

"What mess?" Tyler demanded.

"There it is!" shouted Wilson.

Tyler saw the closed door to the control room up ahead on the right, which meant the sphere was just a few meters further.

Wilson put two fingers to his right ear, then to the air he ordered, "Lieutenant Torres, Lieutenant Washburne, hold your positions as long as possible. The E-R Bridge will not open for another two hours. You both know the importance of this mission. Make us proud!"

The Wilson group stopped outside the sphere. Tyler noted that only half the number of soldiers were still with them as there were before. One of the platoons must have positioned itself further down the tunnel when Mike wasn't paying attention, and were now down there in the dark somewhere. The other platoon was taking up defensive positions here near the sphere. Some lay on the cold ground, others knelt in open doorways to those dark rooms that had filled Tyler with such dread earlier.

"Copy. Copy," Wilson said to no one visible. "Godspeed to you all!" Then he turned to one of the soldiers near him, who waited patiently, holding a square piece of some dark material. "You're just waiting on us, aren't you?"

"Yes, sir," the soldier replied.

"Everyone inside!"

The women ducked into the sphere through the rudimentary hole Tyler had cut in its door earlier. Wilson followed, sitting down and scooting on his rear to negotiate the opening. "My knees," he said. "Don't laugh."

After the Colonel was through, Tyler rolled through the hole, and helped Wilson back to his feet. Behind them, the soldier placed the piece of flat material over the hole, and the sound of welding ensued. *Would that be enough to—?*

An ear splitting, alien sound nearly brought Tyler out of his skin. Hannah and Amber both stood at the edge of the catwalk, their rifles pointed downward, white hot plasma with a greenish tint bursting from their barrels. He walked to the edge and looked down just as they ceased fire. The Hellhound he'd encountered before now lay in a million smoking pieces part-way up the curving wall of the sphere.

"And that's how you take care of wild dogs," Hannah said with a smile.

"Wow," is all Tyler could utter. It had climbed further up the wall since he had left it two hours before. He reasoned that, given enough time, the metal monster probably would have reached the catwalk and dragged itself along, following his scent. *A perfect machine of war, unstoppable with the weapons of the Twentieth Century. Forget the laser guns. If I could get one of those dogs back to 1975, and if our boys could engineer more, the Viet Cong would be on their knees in a matter of days.* "Did you have to completely obliterate it?" he asked the women.

"That's the only way to deal with them," Amber replied. "As unstable as their hybrid electro-organic brains are, it's a wonder they haven't taken out Rommel's Army for us."

"Wait a minute, did you say 'organic'? You don't mean to say there's an actual brain inside that head..?"

"Of course there is," Amber said. "The brain and spinal column are coupled to that machine body. What, do you think we've figured out artificial intelligence to this level? These things are way smarter than any robot. They're real dogs, enhanced almost completely with cybernetics. They can smell better, run faster, and bite harder than any natural canine. And it would seem they know what's been done to them. That means these pups are more pissed off than the meanest junkyard dog you've ever seen. They can calculate your escape routes and run through all the various ways they can kill you while they're still sizing you up. Most people who encounter them are dead before the word 'run' goes through their minds." She eyed him up and down. "You're one of the lucky few to live to tell the tale."

The gooseflesh rose on his arm and a shiver tore through him from head to toe. *Or maybe it's best to just stick to traditional weaponry and tech,* Tyler decided. *Like laser guns. And those cool ovens they had in 1985 that could cook a meal in sixty seconds flat. Or those groovy Star Trek flip phones they had in the mid '90s.*

Remembering the last time he was in this room, he glanced back to the corner of the doorway where he had stashed his rucksack earlier. It was still there, his Kevlar perched on top along with his worthless M-16, just as he had left them. Hannah and Amber had begun walking toward the large rectangular window, their powerful flashlights exploring the sphere. His eyes then fell on Wilson, who was staring at Hannah and smiling. Tyler moved to stand by his friend. "What is it?"

"Hannah. She got her first taste of combat at a time when kids in our day and age were worrying about when their decoder rings would come in the mail."

"Yeah, she's pretty good with a zap gun, I know that."

The old man laughed. "Zap gun! Funny, I like it." Then he leaned in close and whispered. "It's little wonder she was able to fly through the U.S. Army's Infantry School and earn her Ranger tab before her twenty-fifth birthday."

Tyler nodded at first, then his brows came together. "*Wait.* What did you just say?"

Wilson cocked his head and spoke to the air again. "Roger, Lieutenant Washburne, thank you." Then he hollered to the group, "They've finished welding a plate to the opening in the door. We're safe. For a little while, anyway."

"Okay, wait a minute, man," said Tyler. "What did you just say about—"

Wilson put a finger to his lips, and Mike shut his mouth.

"Hey," said Amber, her voice echoing in the space. "Is that a blast shield over the window there?"

Tyler looked at where Amber and Hannah were pointing their handheld torches, each several orders of magnitude more powerful than his trusty MagLite. "Huh. I never even noticed that before."

"And this is the guy who is supposed to save history?" Amber quipped.

"Save history?" Mike turned back to Wilson. "I don't understand."

Amber scoffed. "You explain, Dad, we're going to actually *do* something." She and her granddaughter trotted toward the curved window one-quarter the way around the sphere, a solid one hundred and fifty meters away.

Tyler waited until the women were out of earshot. "Okay, *now* can we talk?"

The Colonel nodded.

"What did Amber mean by, 'save history'? What did you mean earlier when you said something about losing me? What is this about Saigon falling, and what did you mean when you said Hannah earned her Ranger tab before she was twenty-five? She's still, what? Eighteen?"

"Sixteen."

"Sixteen! So why did you just say twenty-five?"

"Because in your world she is twenty five," said Wilson.

"Alright look, man, I know we're in the time travel business and all, but you're not making a lick of sense."

Wilson took a deep breath. "Where do I begin?"

"How about begin with the part about losing me? That's kind of sticking in my head right now."

"Right. Okay, look, I don't know how to tell you this, Mike."

"Just spit it out, sir."

The old man stared at Tyler for another moment before he spoke. "My friend, after you left on this mission you're on now, I never saw you again. Not until Hannah brought you to me today."

Tyler's mind raced. *I never returned?*

"You never came back to 1975, Mike. We tried everything we could think of before they shut us down. Days turned into weeks, and you just… never answered our transmissions. We opened that wormhole every day for a month—probably cost the taxpayers millions—but you never came out of that blue mist. Not even a single squelch from your radio."

Tyler stared at the mesh catwalk illuminated in the glow of his MagLite.

"Certain Congressmen over on Capitol Hill, the handful who were privy to what we were doing, started wondering if the loss of some of our best men—seven at that point, counting you, Travelers One and Two, and those we lost in testing—was worth bringing back a few high-tech trinkets that we probably wouldn't be able to figure out how to reverse engineer for decades anyway."

"So no one ever went through again?"

"One person did. Traveler Four."

"Traveler Four? You mean G.I. Joan? Lieutenant Stark?"

Wilson laughed. "Yes, you do remember."

"Well why wouldn't I?" asked Tyler. "I mean in my timeframe I just saw her yesterday. She sat in on my mission brief and nearly took it over, remember? You were there! She quizzed me on everything. Three times! And you just sat there and let her!"

The old man smiled. "Yes, I remember. Vaguely. Well, Mike, when that girl gets on a roll, it's best to stay out of her way."

"I swear that bitch can see right into my soul. She gives me the heebie jeebies."

Wilson nodded. "Yes, well, I told you she was a fighter. Was since the day she was born. And easy on the name-calling." One corner of his mouth turned up in a half-smile.

Tyler stared at his friend. "Wait a second."

"Yes," said Wilson. "You understand now, don't you?"

He shook his head. "No."

"Yes, you do!"

Tyler looked back at the women, who were busy near the large, rectangular window. "That's impossible." He turned back to the Colonel. "You mean that teenage girl who popped in right out of the blue the day the system was turned on, back in '65, carrying all that advanced tech, is—?"

"Yes!"

"But… But… How in the hell?"

"I don't know, Mike, but I have a theory. You wouldn't remember this part, you hadn't joined the program yet, but I was there. The clothes she's wearing right now? Those are the exact same clothes that little teenager was wearing when she appeared on that platform all those years ago. Believe me, it's her. And this has to be the day she leaves us."

"But she's—!" Wilson's finger went to his lips again, and Tyler brought his voice down to a whisper. "But she's your great granddaughter!"

"Yes, she is. And she's also Lieutenant Stark. Traveler Four."

Tyler shook his head again. "No. No, that's even more impossible."

"Okay, Mike, think about it. That little sixteen-year-old girl remained in government custody and joined the military as soon as she was allowed to. She went on to be the first woman in the combat arms. Off the record of course; the public of that era never got wind of it or they would have thrown a fit. Anyway, since she was literally born into our world as the result of a secret government program, naturally Washington kept her existence a secret. Not hard to do when a person pops out of a wormhole with no birth certificate, no social security number, and no history of ever existing."

"I might not have been there that day, but I and everyone who works here knows that little girl's name was Kara, not Hannah."

Wilson smiled. "She was always smarter than everyone around her."

Tyler stared at the back of the girl's head. Now seeing her with new eyes, from a different perspective, everything about her matched the photos and old film reels he was shown during his initial training. *Wilson was right. He had to be.* "I... I just can't believe it. I refuse to believe it."

"Believe it. It all matches up, now that I look back," said the Colonel. "She was overly nice to me. Oh, she dropped so many hints back then. All of them went completely over my head, of course! She would joke how 'odd it was' that she and I looked so much alike, and she often told me stories of her grandfather 'back in the war'. I naturally assumed she was talking about World War II, but now that I've personally been through all of the same experiences she described, I now know she was referring to me, her *great* grandfather, in *this* war." He smiled. "She was clever. She left out all mention of anything like Hellhounds and exoskeletons and drones and plasma rifles and all the other cool gadgets we now have."

"You've got to be kidding me, man."

"She told me on so many occasions how much she loved her grandpa, who I supposedly reminded her of." He laughed. "Of course, being the young stud I thought I was, I took it all to mean she had a thing for me!"

"Oh, Wilson, come on!" Tyler exclaimed.

"Oh, Mike, nothing ever happened! In fact, she was very firm with me on dating from the start: there was to be *absolutely none of it.* A young Captain Wilson reluctantly accepted the blow to his ego—eventually—and merely enjoyed her company. We shared lots of meals in the cafeteria and talked about her family. I know you were a bit afraid of Lieutenant Stark, but believe me, Kara was—is—a wonderfully warm and incredibly intelligent person. And a bit of a sneaky little..." His voice trailed off.

Tyler had no clue how to process this new information. For the moment, he decided to just go with it. He reminded himself yet again that the term "Time Relocation Mechanism" was something he discussed at a job he reported to every single day. *You big dummy,* he chided himself, quoting a famous sitcom character of the '70s. *What Wilson is proposing is entirely possible. Just... far out. Way far out.* "When did you know?"

"It wasn't until Hannah was about ten that something triggered inside me. It was something in her eyes. By the time she was thirteen, I knew."

Tyler lowered his own eyes. "For the record, I wasn't exactly *afraid* of her, I was— Well, she's scary."

"She can be," Wilson agreed.

The distant sound of plasma fire seeping through the covered hole in the door brought them both back to the task at hand. The battle for the sphere had begun.

"Uh oh," Wilson said. "We're out of time. Listen, Mike, very closely... Kara had her own set of TRM missions, and you yourself had several trips scheduled after this mission to 2075. But all those were postponed indefinitely after we lost you, and the effort to figure out what went wrong took priority. The director wouldn't allow us to continue until we figured out the puzzle, which we never did. And then, one day, the call came to close up shop."

"That must have been the worst."

"Boy, you can say *that* again," said the Colonel. "I saw it as Capitol Hill just... just leaving you for dead. I was livid. There was a lot of yelling. A *lot*. I don't know how General West let me get away with it. He didn't want the program shut down any more than I did, but of course he couldn't allow gross insubordination, either. I threatened to do him a favor and resign my commission before he could drop an Article 15 or a Court Martial in my lap, but then the General opened my eyes. He said, 'there's the door, Matt, but keep in mind you can't fight *The Man* from the outside.' That made perfect sense to me. So I shut up, he somehow found it within him to not punish me for calling him every name in the book in front of the entire staff, and we started coming up with a plan on how we were going to convince the Powers-That-Be to reinstate our baby that we built from quite literally the ground up."

"But I guess it didn't work out too good, huh?" Tyler said flatly.

"Well, something crazy happened that really threw a wrench into things. Not even one hour after we were told to shut down the program, Kara Stark took over the control room, defied every order to stand down, and stepped through an unauthorized rift. She must have been planning it the entire time and was ready to go at a moment's notice."

"What? But how could she do that? She would need the whole control room crew to—"

"She only needed three people, Mike. One to initiate the system startup, one to run the coordinates computer, and one to monitor and compensate for power fluctuations. All the other positions are really there just for redundancy. You know, safety and managerial over-watch. Government efficiency," Wilson said with a smirk.

"Where did she go?"

"Never found out. And here's where the program was finally shut down for good, without any help from Capitol Hill. The shape charges she planted and programmed to detonate exactly one minute after she was gone took care of the navigation computer and all the memory banks, as we called them back then. Left the entire TRM system in shambles. Never got it working again."

"But I got here okay. So something's working."

"Oh, with the lightning rods in place, the sphere can receive no problem," agreed Wilson. "It just can't *send* without a nav computer or without a way to spin the blades."

"Got it," Tyler said. "But surely there were backup memory banks to analyze? To see where she went?"

Wilson let out a breath. "She was very thorough. Having almost grown up around the equipment, she knew those systems inside and out. All the tapes were worthless."

"What about the operators? Surely they talked with enough… persuasion?"

"They were whisked away and I never saw them again. Yes, I'm sure they were interrogated ad nauseum. But if the government bubbas found out anything, they kept that to themselves. And Mike, there's something else."

"Oh man, there's more?"

"She took the journal with her."

Tyler frowned. "What journal?"

"Tesla's."

His jaw dropped. "Not *the* journal? The one they used to develop the time machine in the first place?"

Wilson nodded with pursed lips.

"But how? That thing was locked up God-knows-where!"

"God and Kara both knew, it seems. She even left a note behind in its place. I wasn't privy to what it said, but I hear it was polite." The Colonel shook his head. "But I don't know if any of it even matters. Hell, with the shortcuts she took to initialize the TRM, she may have gone absolutely nowhere. I hope she did, though. Sometimes when I daydream, I imagine she found a way to go somewhere, some*when*, where she could make a difference."

"Well if she went to the future, I'm not sure she made much difference by the looks of *this* place."

"She could have gone further," Wilson said, staring off into the distance. "Maybe a thousand years further. We know this facility lasts that long. Back in the day—when you and Traveler Two were still making regular jumps—we were able to get TRM 'locks' as far out as the year 3000. This sphere may exist for thousands of years beyond that, but we hadn't yet checked past that. Anyway, I have no idea where she went, but I like to entertain the notion she went to the past, not the future."

"The past?" Tyler chortled. "Well that's about impossible. She could only go back as far as 1965, and someone would have seen her pop in; the sphere was manned twenty-four hours a day."

"Yes, that's true. People could have been bribed to keep quiet about a visitor, but it would've been hard to doctor all the myriad data tapes to hide it."

"And we learned right off that you can't go back to a time earlier than when—"

"Yes, there is that," Wilson interrupted. "But I decided a long time ago, pardon the pun, that *anything* is possible, given enough permutations—"

The Colonel was cut off mid-sentence when shouting and plasma discharges erupted directly on the other side of the door to the sphere. Tyler spun, but only saw the dark plate in place over the hole he had cut only two hours before. It now seemed like days ago. He felt helpless. "What can we do?" he asked.

"Nothing," said the old man. "Wait for the wormhole to open."

"This is killing me, not being able to fight," said Tyler through clenched teeth. "Colonel, this Rommel fellow... Tell me this isn't Erwin Rommel, the 'Desert Fox'. The premier General of the Third Reich and Hitler's—"

"Why do you think it's Erwin Rommel?" Wilson interrupted. "Just because we have a time machine?"

"Well, duh."

"Oh! Hold that thought!" Wilson unzipped a small bag he had been carrying around his waist. "How could I have forgotten?" He held up a small transparent orange box, about three inches square and one inch thick.

"What is that?"

"*This* is the three-hundred year history of the United States that I complied myself, from 1776 to 2076," said Wilson. "There are hundreds of documentaries and thousands of news reports and interviews stored on it."

"2076?"

"I just rounded to an even three hundred, it actually only goes to 2075. Don't tell anyone."

Tyler chuckled. "Alright, but what *is* it? Some fancy new tape? How do I play it? Or is it one of those—what did they call them in the early part of this century? A compact disc? DVD?"

"No, no, it's a completely self-contained holographic— You know what? Nevermind. It's like a mini film studio with its own screen and projector." Wilson handed it over.

"Alright." Tyler turned the device over in his hands and didn't see any controls. "How does this thing work?"

"You just talk to it. It's called a 'ProPlay'. Short for Projector Player. You call it by name, and just tell it to play, fast forward, rewind, pause, whatever, and it'll do it. Hannah figured out how to use these things when she was four, so I'm sure you can figure it out."

"Okay."

"I'm giving you two." The Colonel pulled a second one from his bag, only this one was a transparent royal blue instead of orange. "One for the U.S. Government, and one for you to hide. If the government handles it like I think it will, it'll hoard every petabyte for itself, to try to get a leg up on every other country in the world. So I want you to take steps to ensure as much of this information as possible makes it into the public's hands. Once it finds its way to the Internet, you can relax; it will spread all on its own to all four corners of the Earth."

"Um, okay…"

"Mike, the world needs to know how all this happened," the old man said. "The petty differences and arguments of the far Left and far

Right eventually led to the demise of our country. Protests. Riots. Declarations of secession by various states. The country was split in two along political party lines, and America was torn apart by a civil war that continues to this day. The U. S. military was spread so thin that after a while, units were either filled with soldiers performing duty at no pay, or they were simply disbanded entirely. Police forces across the country were strained way beyond their limits. It wasn't long before gangs took over the big cities, and fought amongst themselves over something they couldn't control. It was chaos. Thugs, radicals, religious nuts, regional tyrants... all came out of the woodwork. What used to be minor, harmless political groups were suddenly emboldened. Terrorism ran rampant. The highways were suicide to travel on; fuel tankers and food trucks were the big targets, but every car held something the hijackers wanted. If it wasn't supplies, it was the women. People fought, but they were usually outnumbered. Our medical facilities were overwhelmed and we ran out of medicine pretty quickly. Water and electrical infrastructures eventually crumbled. Those who did survive were killed by their own neighbors for a can of food or a mouthful of water. People were afraid to leave their homes, and even when they did, there was little food and other supplies to be found. Only hunters. Predators preying on the weak."

Tyler listened as the sounds of battle behind him grew louder. He wished he could help. Having to remain safely behind a barricade while American soldiers were dying made him anxious and angry, no matter what time period they were from. But he had his own set of orders that didn't include meeting the enemy head-on. Not yet, anyway. *Stay focused, Sergeant,* he told himself.

"Civil War II created unrest not just in America, but everywhere across the globe," Wilson continued. "Economies were strained, especially in countries that traded heavily with America or counted on us for food, medicine and military support. I hear Europe and Asia are in bad shape economically, but it's hard to get reliable reports with the Internet down. Not a single continent was unaffected. Well, except Antarctica. The penguins learned long ago how to live in harmony."

Tyler didn't smile at Wilson's attempt at humor.

"About ten years before Hannah was born, this Rommel fellow took over, and ushered in an era of relative peace. Took care of most of the gangs, anyway; made going outside not such a suicidal endeavor. I don't know if it's *the* Erwin Rommel, Mike, or just some delusional copy-cat radical who likes the title 'Field Marshal'. All I know is, this guy's bad news. If he has his way, the world will bow to him. And by the way things are going, he may get it. The world isn't doing so well, Mike. One big reason is," here Wilson held up his plasma pistol, "this technology he's got? These weapons? They're not from 2075."

"What?"

"We obtained these guns from raids and dead enemy soldiers. Those Hellhounds? I've never seen anything like them, not in any of the Pentagon's most top secret project development plans I had access to. Not even *DARPA* was working on anything like that, far as I ever knew."

But D.A.R.P.A. was huge, Tyler thought. *They could have been studying anything and everything and the world wouldn't even know about it. Just like the world didn't know about our time machine.* Or at least he hoped it didn't, anyway. *But if Rommel knew...* "Do you think Rommel got these weapons from farther in the future?"

"That's my fear."

Tyler stared at the little orange and blue boxes. "And all that is in these things?"

"All of it. Show the world, Mike Tyler. Future generations must learn how to live together, or they will learn what's it's like to die together."

Tyler swallowed hard, then nodded. "Right. I got it."

"This is your mission now, Mike," Wilson said. "No more futuristic technology needs to be put in the hands of those who don't yet know how to properly wield power. Your job now is no longer to bring advanced tech back home to help the United States win wars. It's to help our country—while it's still healthy and intact in your time—stop the one war that will tear it, and possibly the world, apart."

He nodded again. "I'll do my best."

"I know you will," said the old man. "Oh and one more thing. Hannah's going with you."

Tyler's jaw set. "How did I know you were gonna say that?"

"You see, Mike—" Wilson paused a moment when the sounds of screaming pierced the thin panel behind him, but took a deep breath and soldiered on, speaking faster now. "Hannah is of the understanding—and I tend to agree with her—that if you return to the past and are successful in preventing this civil war from ever happening, she'll never exist."

"Why wouldn't she?"

"She was born after the U.S.A. collapsed. My other great grandchildren were born before. They were..." Here the old Colonel's words stumbled, and he closed his eyes and took a moment to himself before continuing. "They were lost in the war, along with Amber's husband, Steven."

Tyler put a hand on his friend's shoulder.

The Colonel's eyes glossed over in the light of Tyler's MagLite. "I'm alright," the old man said. He took a couple of quick breaths, let it out, and calmed himself.

"So their names aren't Wilson," Mike noted.

"No. Their last name is McAffee. Steven McAffee was a good man, and he and Amber raised a brave fighter named Thomas, their only child. Only after Thomas and his wife Rose lost their other children did they decide to have another. So were it not for this war, Hannah's siblings likely never would have died when they did, and it's entirely possible she would never have been born."

"Wow. That's pretty deep, man."

"Yeah, pretty deep," Wilson agreed.

The two men stood a moment without speaking. The sounds of combat were right upon them. Tyler wondered how much time they had left to spend together. Would they last until the rift opened again? Somehow he doubted it. "What happened to her father? What happened to Thomas?"

Wilson swallowed. "I'd rather not say."

"Okay." Tyler heard an explosion on the other side of the door, likely a grenade. The enemy was 'at the gates'. "I just have one last question, sir."

Wilson blinked the tears away. "Shoot."

"What the hell is the *Internet?*"

Wilson's face scrunched up. "Surely I told you on your visit to—" Before he got any further, a scream came from one of the women.

Tyler's head snapped in their direction. In the light of Amber's flashlight, a Hellhound stared into the sphere from the control room.

"It's okay!" Wilson shouted. "It can't get through the glass! It's not really glass, remember? It's transparent metal!"

"But given two hours, can it get to us then?" Tyler asked in a low tone.

The old man said nothing.

The metal dog in the control room opened its mouth, but its roar could scarcely be heard inside the soundproof sphere. It scratched at the faux glass, then pounded its head into the window. Hannah yelped at the sudden movement. The next instant, the beast seemed to blossom into blue and white fireworks, falling to one side. But it wasn't dead. It trudged upright, turned, and pounced at something in the doorway of the control room. *One of our soldiers, no doubt.*

"I got it! Stand clear, Hannah!" Amber shouted. The heavy metal blast shield fell into place with an ear-splitting concussion that rippled across the expanse of the sphere.

Hannah's beam turned toward them after the artificial thunder had died down. "Now what, Pawpaw?" she hollered.

"Now we wait!" her grandfather hollered back.

"For two hours?" she asked.

"The soldiers will keep at bay the hounds and drones and whatever else Rommel throws our way."

"For two hours." Hannah's tone told Tyler she didn't believe a word of it. "Pawpaw, once the fighting starts, this battle will be over in more like two minutes. Just like all the others. Sixty men aren't going to be enough."

"She's right," agreed Amber. "By now Rommel's Intel Division has put two and two together. He may even know what we're up to. If that's the case..."

"Everything will be okay. I've been planning this for a century now! I have everything covered."

"Except for two covered main entrances and a locked hatch," Tyler said, eyeing the Colonel.

Wilson gave him a look that said, *Quit scaring the women, you idiot.* "If there's one thing my grandmother Ellie Wilson taught me, it was—" Growls and desperate cries filtered into the sphere through the thin piece of alloy welded to the hole in the door. Wilson pointed across the expanse. "Everyone head to the far side!"

The girls simply stared.

"It's the best place in here to mount a defense! Go ahead, ladies! We'll be along in a minute!"

The women began the long jog around the circumference of the sphere.

"Mike, it's time to retrieve your rocketpack."

"Roger." As Tyler turned, a bluish glow lit the room. His eyes rose and found the blue-violet glow of Saint Elmo's Fire. *Already?* He looked at Wilson.

"Time?" the old man shouted.

"Thirteen fourteen!" Amber shouted as she ran. In military time, that meant fourteen minutes past one in the afternoon.

"Too soon," Wilson whispered.

The buzzing of the rods began. With the fire and the buzzing always came the vortex. Tyler's eyes shot to the center of the sphere. Sure enough, a cloud was forming. A red one, indicating a doorway to the past. The occasional lightning bolt shot into it—or from it, Tyler could never figure out which—from one of the countless lightning rods around them. Minus those the hellhound destroyed during its death-throes, and those probably melted by the women's plasma weapons, of course. No matter; the others would compensate. To a point. "That's not for me, is it?" he asked, donning the rocketpack.

Wilson shook his head. "No. Can't be. It's too early. Perhaps... perhaps this is why you never answered our calls?"

"What do you mean?"

"Maybe you flew into this wormhole instead of waiting for ours?"

"Why would I do that?"

"Exactly. Why would you, indeed? No. We'll wait until fifteen hundred. I saw Johansen personally schedule that return rift for exactly 15:00 and initiate it. It's coming. We just have to wait for it."

"But what if this one stays open until then?" Tyler asked. "For another... hour and forty-five minutes, or however much time is left?"

"It won't. As you know, it takes enormous power to keep an Einstein-Rosen Bridge open. It will shut down in a few minutes, max."

"Okaaay. And then if another wormhole opens? And another?"

"We'll wait and see," Wilson said, with a finality to his tone that Tyler could not mistake.

"Roger, boss."

Wilson was silent for a moment, then added. "Mike, if you want to be sure it's not our people calling, get on your radio. Call RAVROCOM."

Of course! Tyler chided himself. His finger flew to his ear to initiate a broadcast. But the button wasn't there. He looked down and found his radio cord dangling from the side of his rucksack. His helmet! His head spun back to the corner where it and his rifle was stashed. Mike jogged the few short steps to the wall, scooped up his Kevlar, yanked the headphone device from it, and dropped it on the catwalk. By the time he walked back to the general vicinity of the Colonel, Tyler had it on his head and plugged into his ruck where the guts of the radio were housed. "Raven Rock Command, this is Traveler Three, over."

No reply.

"Raven Rock Command, Raven Rock Command, this is Traveler Three, over."

Not even a crackle over the airwaves. Only cracks of lightning, the buzzing of the glowing rods, and the final sounds of a battle his side was losing. Or had already lost.

Then Tyler did hear voices, but they weren't coming from the radio. He looked across the sphere and saw the women pointing at them and cupping their hands to their mouths. "Colonel? I think the women are calling to us."

"Say again, sweetheart!" called Wilson. "We can't hear—"

Directly behind them, the patched hole exploded inward. The shining chassis of a Hellhound flew by Tyler, grabbing Wilson in its jaws as it tumbled into the depths of the sphere.

"Wilson!" But his friend was already out of sight. Tyler reached for Betty, but the dog exploded in a blinding flash that knocked him off his feet. He landed on his hands and knees upon the catwalk. Through the wire mesh he watched as both women unleashed everything they had on the mechanical beast below him.

"No," he panted. "Matt—"

Faint curses and screams from the other side of the sphere reached his ears when the gunfire finally came to a halt. Then another sound from behind him froze every muscle in his body. The low growl sent his heart into his throat. If the dog had a breath, it would be warm on his neck.

For whatever reason, the thing hadn't attacked yet. Was it confused as to why he hadn't yet turned its way or fled in horror? Was it waiting for him to reach for his weapon, so it could make the kill in a more animal-like fashion? He had just learned these things were living creatures, after all.

He figured he may be blessed with a single move before the hybrid machine pounced. Out of sight of the dog, Tyler's hand enveloped the small handgrip at his belt. When he mashed the button, the rocket nozzles shot out either side of his rucksack, ignited, and launched him forward into the abyss. Tyler jerked his legs under him and *felt* more than heard the mechanical jaws snap mere inches away. He didn't look back until he was high in the air. When he did, he saw that two more hounds and what looked like a tiny helicopter had joined his newest friend. *That must be a drone. Are those missiles on its underside?* He glanced at the women, who had just begun to unload on the new arrivals now that he was out of the way. He gunned the flight stick forward, aiming for the green and yellow pulses of plasma coming from the women's direction.

Hannah and Amber took out the drone first, probably because it was actually shooting back at them. Tyler considered it a lucky break the dogs weren't outfitted with weapons of their own. Their jaws and claws were enough to deal with! The hounds were now galloping at tremendous speed around the equator of the sphere, from both directions. Amber and Hannah turned out to be crack shots; the dogs were soon tumbling off the catwalks in millions of fiery shards of metal, plastic and bone.

"Tylerrr!"

It was Hannah. Mike had not forgotten what Wilson had said about taking her with him. He steered around the swirling galaxy-like-structure in the center of the room and dove toward the girl. She was now firing again toward the sphere's door, at whatever new threat had appeared in the hole. The small opening made for a nice "choke point" for enemy dogs and machines entering the room, limiting entry to one evil machine at a time.

Before he reached her, the outer ring began to rise upward to meet him. It wasn't a sudden movement—each ring must have weighed a ton—so it wasn't a surprise per se, more of a curiosity. It was surely not moving under its own power; more likely something had hit it and caused it to tilt. He maneuvered up and over it easily. When he was almost directly above Amber and Hannah he started his descent, and spun himself so he could see behind him toward the entry door. His eye caught a glimpse of a Hellhound falling from the other side of the smooth ring and tumble into the bowels of the sphere. He chuckled. "Stupid mutt!" The ring creaked to a halt, now stuck in its tilted position. The action of the dog leaping the ten meters or so to the outermost ring actually helped the humans. With the axis mounts of the outer ring on the north-south ends of the sphere, there was now a large, curved shield partially protecting them from direct laser fire, at least from the direction of the entryway.

With the ring lifted, Tyler had a wide view of the bottom of the sphere. The dog that fell was negotiating the lightning rods below them, quite swiftly at that. "Hey!" Tyler shouted, now just a couple of meters above the women. Amber looked up. He pointed to the dog, and she dispatched it promptly with a salvo of white and green energy. In another few seconds, Tyler landed on the catwalk to Hannah's left.

"I thought you were going to fly into that cloud and leave me!" she yelled over the plethora of sounds echoing in the cavernous space.

"Something tells me I'd rip spacetime a *new one* if I did that," he yelled back, mainly to himself.

"What?"

"Put your arms around my neck and stand on my feet!"

Amber ceased fire for a moment and turned to look in their direction. Tears streamed down her cheeks. "I love you, Hannah!" she shouted.

"I love you too, Grandma!"

Amber blasted a small, spider-like drone that had silently crept up behind Tyler and Hannah.

Tyler's mind reeled. *Wait, there are mechanical spiders, too!?*

"Go! Get out of here!" Amber screamed.

Her salt and pepper mane blocked Tyler's view of her face as she resumed her unending barrage at the army of machines now flooding the sphere. She wielded a rifle in one hand and a pistol in the other, dealing chromatic death in all directions. She looked like a heroine from an action movie, Tyler thought, admiring her.

"I'll come back for you!" yelled Hannah. "I swear it!"

Amber didn't reply. She was focused on keeping the enemy at bay. *At least long enough for us to escape,* Mike thought. *What a brave, honorable woman.*

Tyler launched himself and Hannah upward, just as an explosion rocked the catwalk at the very spot they had just left. The girl turned and sent dozens of plasma bolts toward the drone that had targeted them. Only one bolt nicked it, but it was enough. The drone spiraled out of control and out of sight.

Mike aimed for the swirling vortex at the center of the sphere. Lightning fired off all around him, lasers swept by, plasma bolts zoomed past. More drones fell out of the sky or simply vaporized thanks to Amber's marksmanship skills. Tyler saw dogs snarling and snapping their powerful jaws all around the sphere now. He was thankful there was too much noise to hear their howls. The stench of cordite, hydraulic fluid, smoking machinery, and organic matter from the dogs assaulted him. As he and Hannah darted into the red cloud, Tyler decided it was a stench he never wanted to smell again.

The familiar white light washed over him, and all was in slow-motion once again. A memory zipped through Mike's mind, and he was able to glance down at Hannah while inside his Disney Land. When they entered the sphere, she was in profile to him, her pretty face scrunched up as she shot at targets, her eyes wild in seeming madness. Now, her face was still oriented toward his right, one arm around him, one aiming the rifle. And there they were.

Her skull and jawbone.

He could see right through her skin, just like an x-ray, just like that scientist said all those years ago. He hadn't been lying, and it wasn't a rumor. The Tyler Light was real.

A smile burst across Mike's face the moment they reached the other side.

Tyler immediately pulled back on the handgrip to stop their forward advance. A TRM was creating this wormhole—if not his own in 1975, some other mechanism—and the last thing he wanted was to escape the hell they had just left, only to be sliced to mincemeat by the blades surely waiting to greet them. Magnificent bolts lightning more numerous than Tyler had ever seen surrounded them. Behind them, lasers found their way out of the swirling smoke. One seemed to slice across them, and he was thankful for the rucksack on his back. "Shut it down! Shut it down!"

The vortex sputtered and died away, but the lightning remained stupendous. The arcs seemed to originate not from lightning rods as Tyler had expected, but from six large, silver orbs atop tall pillars spaced equally apart. Crackling and an overpowering hum was all he could hear. The tinny scent of scorched metal replaced the terrible stench of a moment before. The stench of 2075.

But *when* were they now?

The arcs of light subsided with each passing second, and Tyler was able to finally look past the light that enveloped him and Hannah. He couldn't make out much in the darkness, only shadows; some boxy, some round. One thing was certain. They were not in the Raven Rock facility.

Not even close.

IV

The blades began to spin down. The three spinning rings were much closer than Tyler was used to. Using the rockets, he turned himself and Hannah around slowly, taking in this different TRM apparatus, unsure who might be behind its controls.

"Greetings, Sergeant Tyler, Miss McAffee!" a voice said.

Mike looked around for a familiar face. Perhaps this was 1975 after all, just a different facility. But was that possible? Could *Enter* and *Exit* coordinates be moved? He let up on the rocketpack's controls, and he and Hannah settled onto a platform much smaller than that in Raven Rock. As the three strange-looking blades came to a stop and locked into place in concentric rings around the platform, a thought struck him, and every muscle in Tyler's body seized up. "How do you know this girl's name?" he called into the dark.

The platform lowered to the ground, but Tyler and Hannah remained suspended in the air.

"Please, come down from there!" It was the disembodied voice again. "I assure you that you are in no danger."

"You may have been expecting me, but you couldn't possibly have been expecting *her*! Who are you? Where are we?"

"I will greet you properly in just another moment! Please, turn off your flying machine."

Tyler could think of a thousand reasons not to do so, but he admitted to himself he was using at least one and a half times the fuel holding himself and Hannah aloft, rather than just his own body and his equipment. He only had enough fuel for a few more minutes of flight time, if that; he had already used so much already. If he needed it for an emergency later... *Damn,* he muttered, and lowered them to the platform, which was now the ground. Or rather, on the floor of what looked like—from the occasional flash of lightning that still danced between the six orbs—a warehouse.

As if on cue, lights around the room snapped on. Hannah gasped.

What is this place? A museum of some kind? Everything just looked... old. "Hello?" Tyler called.

The sound of turning dials and switches being thrown emanated from behind a tall sheet of steel with a dark, narrow slit running its width. Someone was back there.

Mike was losing his patience. "Hey! Show yourself!"

A thin man in a dark gray suit stepped into view. He walked toward them with some trepidation. "Absolutely extraordinary!" He stopped, spread his arms, and smiled. "Welcome to the Nineteenth Century!"

The crackling stopped completely, the hum died away, and Tyler realized his thrusters were still partially operational. He jammed his thumb on the red, glowing button, and the small rockets shut off and snapped once again back into his rucksack. He let go of Hannah, but she remained close, still hugging him. "Where are we? Who are you? And I need a serious answer as to *when* we are."

The man walked closer. He was tall, about two meters. Dark hair, neatly kept. Still smiling, he said, "Well, the answer to your first question is: you are in my lab in Colorado Springs. As to exactly *when* you are, I already gave you a serious answer. As to who I am, I am Nikola. Nikola Tesla. Pleased to make your acquaintance."

Tyler stared at the man. He looked around the room. If this was some joke Director Johansen or a young Major Wilson was playing, it was definitely elaborate. And definitely not funny. "That's impossible." He stammered. "The TRM doesn't work that way. It only works back to the day it was first powered up."

"Yes, that's true. Or so I'm told. I'm still learning about this technology myself!"

Tyler's brows furrowed. "Still learning? But you're the one who came up—"

"Don't worry, everything will be explained to you, just as it was to me," said Tesla. "But not right now. Right now there is no time. Right now, young Miss McAffee, I must bid you farewell much too soon."

"What?" asked Hannah.

"What?" asked Tyler.

Tesla turned and disappeared behind the steel wall, and switches and dials were manipulated once again. "If we don't reinitiate my TRM in the next few minutes," he said, "we will be forced to wait another twelve hours for the capacitors to charge up. And frankly, when my colleagues in town wake up in the morning, they will surely not be very pleased with the amount of energy I've already used tonight, let alone what I'm about to use initiating a *second* rift in the ether. We need to finish this operation promptly."

"What operation?"

The clicking stopped for a moment. "You know, I haven't chosen a name for it yet. Hmm. Oh I know! We'll call it, 'Operation 1965'."

Tyler caught his breath. "1965!"

"Yes. That's where Miss McAffee is headed. Sergeant Tyler, may I inventory your backpack, please?"

Tyler's jaw still hung limp when Tesla reached him. Without thinking, he removed his ruck and handed it to this stranger claiming to be the famous scientist whose ideas brought the Tesla Project into being. *But not for decades to come.* Tyler's mind raced trying to work out this new conundrum.

The rucksack fell through the well-dressed man's hands, and it thumped hard on the tile floor. "My, my! And you carry it so effortlessly!" Tesla knelt on one knee and rummaged through its contents. He removed the orange film studio—or so Wilson had called it—and a personal computer the people of 2015 had called a "tablet." "You may take the rest, Miss McAffee," he said. "I do beg your pardon, I would pick it up and offer it to you, but it's probably best we just let it lie where it is."

Her face was a mess of confusion.

"And you can keep the impressive weapon you're holding as well," said Tesla. "No place for it here in 1899, that's for sure." He turned to Sergeant Tyler. "Is this all she had with her the first time she arrived in your time?"

"Um, I don't know. I wasn't there. I only saw old film reels."

Hannah's gaze bounced between the two men. "The first time?"

"We'll trust my eidetic memory then," said Tesla. "Not that I was there either, but I have recently been privy to the report. And the films, too. Extraordinary those are, by the way! And coupled with sound!" He headed over to one of the tall pillars and began fiddling with the river of wires leading from it and into the orb high above.

Tyler's mind was scattered. Question after question bombarded him. He didn't even know where to begin. But a few pieces of the puzzle were starting to make sense. Like Hannah. *Or rather Kara...*

She interrupted his thoughts. "But... But..." The girl's mouth opened and closed, and she began to hyperventilate.

Tyler had to focus. Now. "It's okay, Hannah," he assured her, rubbing her arms in an attempt to calm her. "This is how it's supposed to happen. Things are falling into place."

She managed to speak between breaths. "What's falling... into place?"

"Hannah, please, you've got to trust me. If you don't trust *me*, trust your great grandfather. You're a bigger part of this than you could ever realize. Just trust me when I say that if you don't do exactly as Mister Tesla says, you're probably going to cause a paradox that would ripple through time and destroy the whole universe or something!"

"What!?"

"Sergeant!" Nikola chided from across the room.

"Okay, okay," Tyler sighed, "I'm kidding about destroying the universe. But seriously, Time could get really messed up. Please trust me when I tell you that everything will be alright."

Hannah's eyes darted about, and she continued to breathe like the air would be sucked out of the room at any moment.

Tyler hugged her. "It's okay, Hannah. You're going to a safe place."

"Sergeant?" Tesla said, walking back to the platform, "I need to speak with the young lady again."

Mike tried to pull away, but Hannah held tight to his waist. At least her breathing had slowed.

He bent down so their faces were at the same level. "I need you to listen to me very closely. You're not Hannah McAffee any longer. You are *Kara Stark*. Remember that name! Say it with me now. Kara, Sta— you're not saying it with me. Come now, there is no time! Kara—"

"Kara Stark," Hannah blurted.

"Very good!" Tesla said. "If you forget Hannah McAffee ever existed, things will be much easier. Or so I'm told. Now please, just stand right there and don't move. And don't worry about a thing," he added. "I've already done this once successfully, so that means I can do it again."

Hannah's face had turned to stone, and she had gotten her breathing under control.

Tyler wondered if she was just trying to keep from throwing up. "Hannah," he said, breaking her iron grip. He bent down on one knee and held her hands in his. "You're going to really like my time. It's a utopia compared to where you came from!"

"A utopia?" she said. The platform she stood upon began its slow rise into the air on a hydraulic lift. "But my father told me about all the social problems of your time. All the wars! Two world wars! Africa, Vietnam, Korea, the Middle East, the Moon! Pawpaw barely made it out of Vietnam and the Middle East alive!"

"Sergeant Tyler?" said Tesla from behind the steel panel. "Might I suggest that you—"

"Right, right!" Mike hopped down from the rising metal circle and looked upward. "Yes, Hann— sorry, Kara—there are wars, but not for a girl your age. There is only happiness and love and music and movies and teenage boys! A life you can't even dream of!"

"Sergeant Tyler, please take eighteen steps backward," Tesla suggested. He pointed to the six tall pillars holding up the large silver orbs.

It was then Tyler noticed the hair on his arms and the back of his neck were standing on end. The air obtained the familiar smell of ionization. The hydraulic stand holding the platform in place lowered, and the metal circle Hannah-Kara stood upon floated in mid-air, suspended in an electromagnetic field.

"Oh and you'll get to see your great grandfather again! Your Pawpaw!" Tyler smiled, still walking backwards.

"Pawpaw?"

"Yes! He's, oh, probably in his early twenties right about now. He should be there when you arrive."

"Mike, don't leave me! I'm scared!"

"Don't be! I've already seen this happen! This is how it's supposed to happen!"

"I don't mean the time travel!" she shouted. "I mean this machine!"

"Oh! Don't worry, I've done this a dozen times! It's perfectly safe!" The rings, smaller versions than what Tyler was accustomed to, began their dizzying dance. He stopped backing up when he was even with Tesla's control station. "Just be careful! You know, that whole Grandfather Paradox thing."

She smiled, but only for a split second. She knelt down upon the platform as the rings spun faster and faster.

Mike's heart went out to her. "You'll see *me* soon, too," he hollered over the rising din. "In about six years!" A second later he added, "Be nice to me!"

"By the way, Sergeant Tyler," Tesla said, "my apologies for not answering your wireless telegraph call and giving you at least some piece of mind."

"Wireless—? Oh you mean my radio transmission?"

"Yes. It surprised both of us! Honestly I hadn't believed radio waves could work that way. I see I have much to learn from you future people. How your future computers calculate extremely accurate quantum eigenvalues is just about the most amazing thing I've ever seen."

One phrase in the babble Tesla uttered stuck in Tyler's gut. *Both of us?*

"You'll forgive me, I'm sure," Nikola went on to say, "I was a little busy these past months building this T-R-M as you call it; I didn't have a lot of time to build a wireless telegraph *transmitter!* You're lucky I even have a receiver." Tesla spoke calmly, as if he were having tea, all the while busily adjusting a myriad array of switches and dials. "But now that I know Maxwell and Hertz were right about radio, and I was... *wrong...* I'll get right on it!" He nearly spat the noun as if suffering an injury. "I may have to eat some of my words, as well. That won't be pleasant."

"Excuse me, Mister Tesla, but did you just say *both* of you?" asked Tyler. He looked around the room. "Is there someone else—"

Lightning discharged upon the rings, recapturing Tyler's attention. He looked around for the lightning rods, for the fires from Saint Elmo he so enjoyed, but saw none. The six orbs seemed to be taking over their job.

A breeze picked up, but one not near as strong as that which rose in the Temporal Sphere. The lightning increased and danced all around the structure, a few arcs straying off into the adjacent walls. Tyler glanced over at Tesla again. The man's eyes flew over gauges and flashing light patterns, all labeled with words Mike couldn't begin to pronounce. They might not even have been written in English; he remembered from his training that Nikola Tesla was fluent in several languages.

The scientist stared at the ensuing chaos through the slit in the large steel wall before him. "Annnnd..."

There was a blinding flash of white light, and Hannah-Kara was gone, replaced by the familiar swirling blue wisp of smoke, lightning darting in and out at random. This vortex was smaller than the others, probably an aspect of this rudimentary TRM apparatus, Tyler decided. *Oh man!* It then occurred to him that he forgot to ask Hannah if she experienced the slow-motion like he did. *Now I'll never get the chance.* The thought bummed him out a little. It was probably his one and only opportunity to share the experience with another soul.

"Just look at it," Tesla said. "A rip in the very ether of space. It's beautiful."

Ether? I thought Einstein called it "spacetime." Hmm. What year was Albert Einstein born in again? A thought entered Mike's mind, and he couldn't believe it didn't occur to him before now. *Wait a second. Can I step through this rift and go home, right this very minute? Or would that create a paradox?* Then another possibility hit him. "Um, Mister Tesla, isn't it dangerous to leave the rift open?"

"I don't think so. Why do you ask?"

"Well, can't someone from 1965 come through as easily as Hannah departed?"

"Oh! Yes! You're absolutely right!" Tesla threw a large switch, and the vortex puffed out of existence. His hands flew over the controls, and the blades began to slow. Angry bolts of electricity still crackled until the energy field collapsed, finally absorbed by the network of steel orbs.

"I have another question, sir," said Tyler. "Is it possible for the U.S. Government to simply re-open a rift right back to here?"

"If I understand this technology correctly—and I'll admit I could be wrong in saying this—but I don't believe so. They can't use their machine to come here from 1965 any more than I can use my machine to travel back to 1865, or any time before I built it. I can go back to May if I wish—when I first powered the apparatus up—but I cannot go back and smother baby Thomas Edison before he ever becomes a waste of air."

Tyler nodded. "Okay," he said. He had no idea how to respond to Tesla's last comment, but he was satisfied with the answer. "So what now? Can you program this thing to take me back to 1975?"

"Not just yet," said a feminine voice from elsewhere in the room. "Right now we need get to work. We have a *lot* to do in the coming months."

Tyler spun around, looking for the source. Footsteps from high heels echoed in the large laboratory. He held his breath. There was something *terribly* familiar about this voice.

A woman in high-fashion for 1899 stepped from behind some large equipment. She gave him a big, toothy smile. "Hello, Mike."

His breath caught, and his heart tried to jump out of his chest. "Lieutenant Stark!?"

"I want to commend you for a successful mission. You didn't let me down."

His jaw worked, but that was about it.

"Even though I remember it all vividly—the battle in the sphere, arriving here with you, my first meeting with the amazing Nikola Tesla—"

At this, Tesla smiled and gave her a wink. She puckered her lips and launched a kiss in his direction. Tyler's jaw was on the floor. His mouth was unable to form words and his brain could barely think in complete sentences.

"—I was still a little worried you might not make it back with me, or rather with my younger self," Kara Stark continued. "You know, Quantum Chaos Mechanics and all."

"Quantum?" Tyler burst. "Chaos?"

"There's a reason I grilled you before you left. Exponential sensitivity. One little deviation could have trickled down the line and the woman standing before you may have ceased to exist!

Even a tiny decoherence value in the equation—" She paused, and her face relaxed. "Forget about it, those are my problems, not yours." She stepped closer and eyed him up and down. "You, know, you really made an impression on me all those years ago, at the tender age of sixteen." Her eyes drifted upward, staring down memory lane, her giant smile growing again. "Ah, schoolgirl crushes. Lucky for you I got over *that one!* But I still remember it like it was yesterday. Funny, it actually *was* yesterday for you!" Her eyes grew wide. "No! It was more like... two hours ago when we first met, wasn't it?"

"How the Hell did you get here?" he blurted, finally finding the words he wanted.

She looked at Tesla. "We can discuss that over dinner. I hear we're having duck!" She turned back to Tyler, still grinning like the Cheshire Cat. "For now, all you need to know is that I'm here, you're here, and we have a lot to figure out if we're really going to try to create that Utopia you just lied to my younger self about."

"What?"

"I'm giving you a new mission. And I don't want to hear any lip, Sergeant! As a commissioned officer, I do outrank you still, no matter what century we're in."

Tyler swallowed hard and remained silent. Could she still order him around? Even in 1899?

"Michael James Tyler," Kara said, stepping unnervingly close, an imposing figure. Her green eyes turned to slits as she looked down at him, her chin held high. Her stare went right through to his soul, and not for the first time. "We're going to stop a war, you and me," she said.

He thought for a moment. "What war? Yours? How do we stop a war here in the Nineteenth Century that won't take place for another hundred and fifty years?"

"Not *my* war," she said, straightening the sleeves of his now wrinkled and sweaty uniform. "All of them."

An overlay of the Raven Rock Mountain Complex
(as of 2016)

Entry "Portals" A and B, plus the Security Center
(lower right)

Site-RT, the radio tower atop Raven Rock

Thank you for reading The Tesla Project: 1975, I hope you enjoyed it!

You can learn more than you ever wanted to know about the real Raven Rock Facility (a.k.a. *Site-R)* by visiting the "About Camp David" Raven Rock Mountain Complex page (link below). Unlike many sites, About Camp David is not a conspiracy or parody site; I'm told only factual, unclassified information is published therein.

http://aboutcampdavid.blogspot.com/2011/08/raven-rock-mountain-complex.html

Additional photos and information can be found on their blog:

http://aboutsiter.blogspot.com/p/site-r-photos.html

A big thank you to the folks at *AboutCampDavid.Blogspot.com* for their permission to include their URLs and resources in this story.

A big thank you to my Beta and "Advance Reader Copy" readers!

Special Thanks to those in **bold**; each of you directly made The Tesla Project what it is today! I am in your debt.

Eric Armstrong
Ian Cahill
Amanda Dickinson
Vern Fraedrich
Laura Fredrickson
J.R. Frontera
Greg Getzoff
Kristin Helling
David Hewitt
Richard Hewitt
Barbara E. Hill
Carrie Lamm-Clark
Dyann Love-Barr
Dana McCormack
Jonathan Mendenhall
Shane Nee-Cowen
David Scarlett
Corrine Sharp
Sean Sherman
Dax Snaer
Cullen Stapleton
Lisa Ward
Christine Whittamore

Dear reader,

May I ask a favor? I would be thrilled if you could hop over to Amazon.com and post a super quick review of the Tesla Project: 1975. Good or bad, either is fine; like I've often said, an honest review is better than a glazed donut any day, **and will help make future Tesla Project stories that much better!** Parts II and III are already in the works!

Also, I entertain all cool sci fi and speculative fiction ideas. e-mail me! rod@rodwerks.net

Rod Galindo
July, 2016

The following is an excerpt from the upcoming full-sized novel "Distress Call", the first in the SENTCORPS military sci-fi series.

Distress Call

Sentinel Corps
Log One

By
Rod Galindo

I

Interstellar Civilian Transport Vessel
Emerald Pearl

A jolt of electricity yanked Rae out of hibernation. She gulped the icy air as if she had just burst to the surface of a deep, dark ocean.

Where am I?

Her arms flailed. She searched for something, anything, to make sense of her world. On all sides, cold metal and glass met her fingers. It was several inches from her face so it was not suffocating. Not yet. Confusion assaulted her mind. If only she could see!

Am I dead?

She breathed deep. Cool, crisp air filled her lungs. She smelled ethyl alcohol. A tanginess offended her tongue.

Calm down, Rae, she told herself. *Calm down. Remember what Mom said. Deep breaths. Breathe in, breathe out, breathe in... Okay. Take stock. Am*

I safe?   She didn't know.   She was breathing, feeling, smelling, tasting. *Maybe not safe, but not dead at least.*

Something pulled at her skin when she moved. It made her cease her frantic movements.   Rae carefully ran a hand up the length of her left arm. She found a small tube and a string. No, a wire. Then another. She discovered several more tubes and wires jutting from her body. A chill ran down her spine. Her breathing quickened. *Pull them out or leave them in?*   She didn't know the answer. Maybe they were keeping her alive?

A yellow flash filtered through her eyelids.

What was that?

Rae held her breath.   A pulsing in her neck matched the thumping in her ears. She tried to open her eyes. An inky blackness surrounded her. Had she succeeded? *Do my eyes not work? Or is it just too dark in here?*

Where is here??

She counted her racing heartbeats to calm herself.

One, two, three—

Another flash.

There it is again!

Her arm dropped to her side, and the familiar texture of clothing brushed against her palm. *Is that my favorite blouse?   The purple one?*   She remembered picking out her favorite top for... for what? First day of seventh grade at her new school? No. Not yet. A trip? Yes, the long trip from—

A sound louder than her own heavy breathing crept into her consciousness. It was an alarm. More specifically, a klaxon, like on a vessel. *That's right. I'm on a ship.* But not at sea. Not this time. The yellow flashing every two seconds now made sense. That, combined with the alarm, meant one thing.

Danger.

I want my daddy. Rae's chest tightened. *Where is Da—*

"*Emergency. Emergency,*" said a lady's voice. It was oddly calm. "*Hull breach detected. Life Support and Environmental Systems at risk of failure. Immediate evacuation recommended. Emergency. Emergency—*"

2

Galactic Sentinel Corps Ship *Nightingale*

Captain Moses Elwick sat at a beat-up gray desk and sipped a cup of stale coffee. He leafed through a sketchbook full of colorful drawings and short poems. Hasty scribbles filled the margins. "For Mom" was scrawled next to some, "For Dad" next to others. Some better explained what the illustration or poem was meant to be about. Turning the pages, he paused on a colorful butterfly. It sparked a memory of a peaceful afternoon at home seven years ago, the last stress-free day he spent with his daughter before once again be shipping off to war. The moisture in his eyes blurred everything. A tear fell onto his lap, making a dark spot on his navy blue tunic.

"I brought a little something," Petty Officer Kelly Graydon said from the other side of the desk. She pulled a chocolate cupcake with pink icing out of a small bag. A holo-candle was jammed into the center. She sat it gently on the desk in front of Elwick.

The little cake looked completely out of place in this cold, military environment. "Oh, Kelly." The sweet smell of sugary icing and chocolate made his stomach growl in anticipation.

"It was Zoey's idea," she said quietly. Kelly touched the side of the candle and it flickered to life.

Moses' chest heaved.

"She still loves ya, ya know."

Elwick said nothing.

"Don't think I haven't noticed what you've been doin' to yerself this past year," his Sister-in-Law said. "Throwin' yerself into yer work won't do the trick. It'll catch up to ya. Probably why you've been havin' trouble with yer tummy lately."

Elwick stared at the faux flame for a long time. "She would have been ten next Friday." He looked up. The hazel eyes of the intimidating red-head stared back at him under her Navy-issue ball cap, already welled up with tears. Graydon's stark features softened to an amazing degree in the light of the candle. Moses watched the holographic flame of the tiny white stick "burn" in an uncannily natural way. It gave off no heat, thus posed no danger of setting off the fire extinguishing systems in the Captain's cabin, but he could have sworn it was the real thing.

Kelly reached two muscular arms across the desk, and covered Moses' hands with hers. "Make a wish for 'er," she suggested. "I know it's not exactly her birthday, but with our hectic lives out here in the Black, there's no tellin' when we'll get this chance again." Her touch was gentle, despite the tremendous potential strength her grease-smudged fingers possessed.

Moses sat for a moment, and tried to come up with something his baby girl might want. Nothing material of course; Alena was above such things and better than that. He nodded to himself when he landed on the perfect wish. With a quick blow, the holographic flame went out exactly as it was designed to do, using the magic of tiny sensors programmed to detect human breath or a strong breeze. Water streamed down his cheeks now. "You know what they say," he began, but choked mid-sentence. His face corkscrewed in a way few had seen.

Still holding one hand, Kelly walked around the desk and put her free arm around him and squeezed tight.

Had it been anyone else but Graydon, Elwick would have choked it all down like strong military men are expected to do. A ship's Captain simply could not show such vulnerability to those who served under him. Or so he was taught in the Navy. But here in his own cabin, among family, he wept openly. He could hear and feel Kelly sobbing quietly above him. "You know what they say about the good," he finally managed to force out. If she gave a non-verbal reply, he couldn't see or feel it.

Moses breathed deep and held it a long moment, staring hard at the little cake in front of him. When he exhaled, he had regained at least some of his composure. "*Deus tecum*, my Angel. Daddy loves—"

"Officer of the Deck to the Captain," a disembodied voice interrupted.

Elwick clinched his eyes and attempted to force the pain and sadness away before he had to speak to one of his men. Since that was impossible, he simply stuffed it back in the dark recess from whence it came for the time being. Seconds later, his eyes burst open and he was in command of his little universe once again. He let go of Kelly Graydon's hand. *Time to get back to work.* To his right, a screen embedded into the dingy, gray desk had illuminated itself. Text poured down the small display at a high rate of speed, and a virtual button labeled "21MC" was illuminated. "Speak of the Devil," he said.

"As I was saying," Kelly smirked.

Moses touched the button activating the Twenty-One Main Circuit, one of dozens of standard communications channels available on naval and some civilian vessels. He now used it to connect his cabin directly and discretely to the bridge. "Elwick." He palmed the tears from his face. "Go ahead, Mister LaRoque."

"Sir, we just received a QE-qué from Deep Space Sentinel 3287. It's an automated distress signal."

"Let's hear it."

"It's text only, sir, and a whole lot of it. I was able to pull out location coordinates, ship registration number, time of—"

"Is that's what's flying across my screen now?"

"Aye, sir."

Moses closed the sketchbook. "Go with the Delta-Lima-Tango."

"Aye aye. Distance: four hundred forty-six point three light years. Time-to-Intercept under Safe Jump Protocol: about three hours. But it's probably going to take longer than that."

Moses stood and lifted his flight jacket from the back of the chair.

"Boy, that's a long ways away," said Kelly.

"Yeah it is," Moe replied. "Safe Jump Protocol be damned; everyone could be dead in three hours. Ozzie can surely get us there in—" *Wait a second.* He paused with one arm into a sleeve. "Lieutenant, did you just say *longer* than three hours? Why? And you skipped the location."

"Well, sir, that's where there's cause for some concern..."

Moses' eyes locked with Kelly's for a moment. "Mister LaRoque, what sector is Sentinel 3287 in?"

"The map says it's assigned to Sector two-four-two Charlie."

"Two-four-two—?"

"Don't bother, sir, I already looked it up. It's immediately inside the Hades Quadrangle."

Moe closed his eyes. *Damn.* He prided himself on having successfully avoided such unpredictable regions of space throughout his entire naval experience, both during his former military career and now his civilian one. If he assumed this mission, he would be forced to dive headlong into an area officially off-limits to ninety-nine percent of the population of the galaxy, and dragging his entire crew in with him.

As if reading his mind, Kelly offered playfully, "Hey, come on, what are them stats again? Somethin' like three in ten ships don't come back? Only three? Eh, we can beat those odds any day!" She smiled.

Moses stared at her and finished donning his flight jacket.

"Right?" She held the smile, but her gusto disappeared.

He looked down at his daughter's book of drawings. *Well, we only live once, don't we, Allie? And such a short time it is.* "Understood, Kyle. Have Mister Floyd begin plotting his jumps."

"Aye aye, Captain, he's already started."

Elwick glanced at the timepiece strapped to his left wrist. Orange digits read "18:46". He had put off evening chow in lieu of a depressing walk down memory lane. Now he'd likely miss dinner altogether. But his stomach would have to wait.

"I'd better get back down below decks," said Graydon. She moved quickly in the direction of the door.

"On my way, Mister LaRoque." Moses said and closed the circuit. "Kelly."

She looked over her shoulder, her hand on the door latch.

"Thank you."

Two long strides later and Graydon was crushing him with a tight hug. Then she regained her military bearing, patted his shoulders with rigor, and disappeared through the only exit to Elwick's quarters.

Moses carefully placed his precious book in a nightstand. "Duty calls, sweetheart. As it always does." He looked up and stared at the words "*DEUS GUBERNAT NAVEM*" above his door for a moment in quiet reflection, then departed his cabin with a purpose.

3

Emerald Pearl

"Emergency. Emergency. Atmospheric System failing. Environmental System failing. Immediate evacu—"

A muffled sound entered Rae's consciousness. It sounded like a voice. But not like the one she had just heard.

"Addy!"

Addy? The voice was louder than the lady making announcements. And that voice was mechanical. Rae guess it was the computer. This voice sounded human, but Rae couldn't be sure.

"Mommy!" came another muffled call.

That one was unmistakable. Her mind found focus, and her eyelids shot open. "Tabby!" she croaked. Rae lunged forward and pushed with all her tiny might. The lid to her hibernation pod rose reluctantly. She tumbled from the coffin-like structure onto the cold floor. The motion pulled hard on the tubes and wires inserted under her skin. She lifted herself to hands and knees, and froze. *Oh no.* Her eyes darted to the many plastic "strings" dangling behind her. No puddles of red or clear fluid pooled on the gray tiles. Built-in breakaway joints on the tubes had allowed her to escape without making a bloody mess of herself. She thanked the Great Mother Nature for what her own mother called "small favors." The yellow light flashed again. Every two seconds… She ignored it.

Rae breathed. It was hard to do so. She couldn't feel her hands, though they were right in front of her. She lowered her head and saw her knees, both legs wrapped in black leggings. She couldn't feel those, either.

Tabby.

Rae tried to climb to her feet. Her legs wobbled like a foal only learning to walk, and she fell back onto her knees. *Why won't my legs work? How long have I been asleep?* She tried again, this time turning in a slow circle back toward the cryopod from which she had recently tumbled, and used it for support. Her arms burned and shook with the effort. Her knuckles turned white as she held onto parts of machinery jutting out from the sarcophagus.

"Ayyyy!"

She looked to her left. *Tabby!*

"Rae, get me out!" Her voice was muffled but Rae could understand her. Her younger sister stood in the partially illuminated stasis pod next to her own, banging away at the curved glass.

Rae dove to the chamber holding her sibling, her arms and legs screaming as a million invisible needles pricked every sinew and tendon. "It's okay, Tabby! I'm here!" Rae dug her fingers into the seam of the door. It didn't budge.

"Get me out of here!"

"I'm trying!" Rae noticed a lit screen to her right. It flashed words she didn't care to read. She pounded on the display, first with her palm, then with her fist. It flashed green, and the glass door hissed. It took forever to rise. Rae flung her arms around Tabitha, but the ten-year-old fell into her, sending both girls to the floor in a heap. The fall made quick work of the tubes and wires that held Tabby prisoner.

The little girl looked around. "What happened? Where's Mommy?"

"I don't know," Rae replied.

Rae now had a full view of the cryogenic stasis chamber as she lay on her back. Visual and audible chaos assaulted her from all sides. And every two seconds it became bright as day. "Wasn't Daddy across—?"

"Daddy!"

Rae looked "up" from her perspective to where Tabby pointed, and waited for the recurring yellow flash. *There!* Their father was indeed in the pod across from Rae's. But it was—

"Mommy!" Rae's head snapped down and she saw Tabby looking at the pod next to her own. In another two seconds she saw their mother's face. Her pod was dark, unlike Rae and Tabby's, each of which glowed with a dim white light in the darkened room. In the flash of the emergency lights, Mother's upper torso was in full display behind the glass of the "coffin."

"Looks like she's not awake yet," Rae said.

"Neither is Jamie."

Rae saw their brother Jamie in a fourth pod, on the other side of their mother. Four others lay beyond his in a small alcove. No, eight more.

"Emergency. Emergency," said the calm lady once again. Her voice echoed in the metal room. *"Hull breach detected. Life Support and Environmental Systems failing. Immediate evacuation recommended."*

Tabitha was off Rae now, enabling her to sit up. She looked over her shoulder toward her father's pod, and saw three others beside his. Her eyes darted back and forth, using the two-second strobe to piece together the entire cryogenic chamber.

The cryopods in her father's row were all dark. The small datascreen jutting out to the right of each pod was also dark. When Rae looked back at her mother's screen, it had several blue, jagged lines plodding across it. Words labeled each line, "Cardiac," "Respiratory," "Neurological," among others. Jamie's was the same, as were the other four next to his. Her father's screen showed none of these things, nor did any of the other seven along his wall. *What does that mean? That they're turned off? Or broken? Surely all eight can't be broken!*

Rae dragged herself to her mother's pod, made her way to her feet, and touched the small screen. Instantly, soft white lights snapped on in the interior of the unit, illuminating her mom's face and chest like Tabby's was a minute before. The light glinted in multiple hues off the diamonds adorning the woman's neck, ears and nose. The pewter Triple Goddess pendant hanging between her collar bones seemed to almost absorb the light that fell upon it, but its center lilac-colored amethyst stone shone with a brilliance Rae had never before seen, and the tiny amethyst stones embedded in the crescent moons on either side of the center circle seemed to sparkle with life. The Wiccan symbol of maiden, mother and crone made Rae smile. Her eyes fell downward upon the sleeveless, forest-green dress her mother wore for the trip. It caressed the floor when she walked. Rae could only see half of it; the metal casing of the pod concealed everything below the waist. Her mom's long, golden hair was pulled to one side as if in a hurry. She did that often, out of habit. It was probably the last thing she did before settling in for the long sleep. *She looks like an angel,* Rae thought. *So peaceful. I almost hate to wake her up.*

The next time Rae looked, the small screen displayed additional information. She read it and navigated through a surprisingly simple menu. It appeared it was possible to interrupt the hibernation process. But each friendly blue virtual button she touched immediately turned an unfriendly red, and a nasty notice appeared on the screen. *"No authorization to perform this function."* She tried various approaches and received similar messages. Mother did not wake up. She didn't even seem to be breathing as far as Rae could tell. But all indicators said she was alive.

Rae limped to her father's pod. Her legs ached with each step, but at least the needles were beginning to disappear.

She touched the small dark screen on his pod several times. Nothing happened. She could see her father's face through the glass that separated them each time the yellow light flashed. He didn't look peaceful like Mother. His face was all twisted up. He was in pain. Rae's heart nearly burst from her chest. She began to cry. "Daddy!" she shouted. But there was no response. Her lower lip quivered.

No...

About the Author

Rod A. Galindo arrived on Earth in the Spring of 1970. He's been trying to stay out of trouble ever since, but has now accepted it as one of the three things he does well, right behind drawing and right ahead of spelling. He's beamed all around the world thanks to various military and government positions, but proudly calls Kansas City home. Mainly because his request for transfer to Stargate Command was denied. AGAIN.

"Major Galindo" has nearly thirty years of service under his belt in the U. S. Army, both Active Duty (as an enlisted M-1A1 Abrams tank crewman, Operation Desert Storm) and the Kansas Army National Guard (as a Field Artillery officer, Operation Noble Eagle and Operation Iraqi Freedom).

"Rod Galindo" is a worn-out father of four; two cyber-smart boys aged 15 and 12, one German Army (Bundeswehr) Soldatin who is as dangerously clever as she is beautiful, and he fills in as full-time father to a special young lady who never really had a dad to call her own.

Rod is a fully assimilated and very active member of the Wordwraiths Writing Collective and Wordwraith Books, LLC (learn more about our authors and books at Wordwraiths.com). Enjoy his shiny art or delve into his literary musings at RodWerks.net or RodGalindo.com.